"And you probably thought watching over me was going to be easy," Allison said, laughing.

"Easy?" Kane held out a hand and helped her up. "Jumping out of a plane is easy, scaling a twelve-foot wall with a thirty-pound knapsack is easy, even digging trenches in a desert is easy."

He tried not to look at her lips, tried not to remember how only a few hours ago they'd been so eager against his own. He saw her eyes deepen to a seductive shade of smoky green. He fought the tightening of his groin.

"But watching you is by far the most difficult thing I've ever had to do."

BARBARA McCAULEY is the author of over thirty bestselling romance novels, including *Blackhawk's Sweet Revenge,* the first volume of her popular SECRETS! miniseries for Silhouette. Her work has been nominated eight times by the *Romance Writers of America* for Best Short Contemporary in the prestigious RITA® Award contest. She has also received numerous "Top Picks" from *Romantic Times BOOKclub,* plus several Best Short Desire and "W.I.S.H." awards for her hunky hereos and two Career Achievement Awards. All of her books have appeared on the Walden books romance bestseller lists. A native of Southern California, Ms. McCauley enjoys spending time with her husband and two children, and working in her garden when she can manage to break away from her computer.

BARBARA McCAULEY

Nightfire

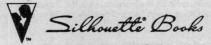

Published by Silhouette Books

America's Publisher of Contemporary Romance

ISBN-13: 978-0-373-47076-1
ISBN-10:   0-373-47076-2

NIGHTFIRE

Printed in U.S.A.

For Judy.
Thanks for being such
a great sister. And for Frank.
Always.

One

He stood at the window, waiting, his gaze dispassionate as he quietly observed the traffic moving over the rain-slicked roads below. When her blue minivan pulled up in front of the twelve-story glass-and-chrome office building he recognized it immediately, just as he knew he would recognize her, though he had never actually seen her before. As if announcing her arrival, lightning split the Seattle sky in a burst of white-hot brilliance and the pursuant crack of thunder rattled the office window.

Five hours ago he'd never heard of Allison Elizabeth Westcott, but now he could tell her what she ate for breakfast, where she shopped for clothes and even where she bought her gas. She was five foot six in her stocking feet, brown hair, green eyes. He knew she had a mole on her left breast 1.6 mm wide, a scar on her right knee from a horseback-riding accident two years ago that had ended her dancing career and a speeding ticket from the Seattle police department. A ticket she'd fought against and won, he noted with a flicker of admiration.

Some people might consider his knowledge an invasion of privacy, but it mattered little to him whether they liked it or not. When he had a job to do, feelings meant nothing to him, his or anyone else's. He simply did what he had to do and made sure no one got hurt.

It was raining hard now and he watched as she darted from her car toward the shelter of the building. It would take her two minutes and forty-five seconds to walk into the room, three minutes, twenty-two seconds if the elevator stopped at every floor.

He stared at his watch and waited.

The storm was already in full force by the time Allison pulled in front of Westcott Pavilion. Raindrops the size of nickels drummed like angry tin soldiers on the hood of her car while a flash of lightning, followed by a distant crack of thunder, promised more to follow.

Allison stared out her windshield at the fierce gray sky, thinking she might wait it out, but the somber note in her father's voice when he'd called St. Martin's Center and requested that she come to his office right away allowed no hesitation.

Drawing a deep breath, she opened her car door and dashed furiously across the sidewalk and through the smoked-glass entry doors, catching enough of her reflection to see that her shoulder-length hair was already a mass of damp, disobedient curls. Some people complained it rained every time they washed their cars. With Allison, it rained every time she straightened her hair.

Twelve stories up the elevator doors opened and she

stepped out, hesitating at the sight of two men in dark suits standing at the outer door of her father's office. Though it was certainly not unusual for employees or clients to be milling about, there was something about the men she couldn't quite place that disturbed her, something that caused a knot to form in her stomach and the hair on the back of her neck to rise. Though she didn't know them, she had the distinct feeling that they not only knew exactly who she was, but that they'd been waiting for her. They continued to watch her as she approached, then nodded stiffly when she moved past them.

Mrs. Harwood, her father's secretary, was on the phone. The attractive brunette looked up from her call, then waved anxiously toward the interior office, mouthing the words, "Your father's waiting."

What in the world was going on? Allison thought, noting the grim expression on Mrs. Harwood's face. The woman always had a smile for everyone. The knot in Allison's stomach tightened a notch.

Her father was sitting at his desk, tapping the polished mahogany top with a silver pen, deeply intent on the paperwork in front of him. She'd always thought he looked more like the football hero he'd once been rather than the president of a computer company—a company he'd started on a dream and five thousand dollars borrowed from a bank he now partly owned. She closed the door behind her. Startled, he looked up from his work.

"Dad, who are those men out in the—"

That's when she saw the other man. He was standing by the corner window, his arms folded across his wide chest, his dark gaze locked on her. Allison faltered, but it wasn't just the surprise of realizing she wasn't alone with her father that had her heart beating faster. It was the intensity of the man's eyes as he continued to stare at her. She held his gaze, at first because a three-foot crowbar couldn't have pried her away, and then as she gained her composure, out of sheer defiance.

His hair was dark as coal, his eyes midnight blue, intensely intelligent and completely void of emotion. There were tiny lines at the corners, most certainly from frowning, Allison figured, based on the hard set of his jaw and lips. And tall. At least six foot three, and even with the sport coat and slacks he had on she could see that he had the distinct build of an athlete: broad shoulders, narrow waist, muscular arms and legs. His stance appeared casual, but Allison felt the vibrations of the energy coiled inside him, and she sensed he could move with the same speed as the lightning that streaked across the sky behind him at this very moment.

Thunder rumbled in the distance.

Allison turned back to her father. "I'm sorry. I didn't know you were with anyone. I can come back—"

Oliver Westcott shook his head. "Come sit, Allison."

There was something wrong, something terribly wrong, Allison realized with icy dread. She hadn't heard that tone in her father's voice since the night he'd called her into his study and told her that her mother had died.

Her legs shook as she moved closer to the desk, but she did not sit. "What is it?"

"Maybe nothing at all," Oliver answered, and his frown softened. "But just to be on the safe side, I've ordered additional security here in the building and brought in Mr. Kane. Kane, this is my daughter, Allison. Allison, Thomas Kane."

"Mr. Kane."

He nodded. "Just Kane will do."

She acknowledged him with a nod of her own, then turned her attention back to her father. She could see he was hedging, and she knew he only did that when he was worried. Really worried. "What 'safe side' are you talking about, Dad? What's happened?"

Oliver sighed, then scooped up the papers on his desk and handed them to Allison. As she took them she realized they weren't papers, but black-and-white photographs. She glanced at them quickly. They were all pictures of her and her father.

"Detective Carlos Fandino of the Seattle police department gave these to me early this morning," he said soberly. "The police lab developed them from a roll of film found under the seat of a stolen car."

She looked at the pictures more closely. The first few shots were of her father coming out of the pavilion. The next three were taken at a restaurant where they'd had lunch together two days earlier. Confused, she continued to move through the pile. There were more shots of her getting into her car after grocery shopping, a few more of her coming out of her apartment.

A cold chill seeped through her as she looked through the pictures. When had these been taken? And by whom? She hadn't seen anyone with a camera or—

She froze as she came to the last picture. It was of her, obviously taken from a distance with a zoom lens. She knew exactly when and where this picture at been taken: last week, the night she'd slept at her father's house after his birthday party. She was sitting at the dressing table in the upstairs bedroom.

And the only things she had on were a bra and panties.

Kane watched Allison as she slowly sank into the chair. Her face, flushed only moments ago from her mad dash out of the rain, turned ghostly white, giving her the appearance of a frightened porcelain doll. Her mouth opened in astonishment, and as he stared at her lips he realized they were wider and fuller than he'd noticed in his ID pictures.

She was much more beautiful in the flesh, he decided, but couldn't quite decide why. Perhaps it was the fire that danced in her brown hair under the fluorescent lights, or maybe it was the shade of green in her eyes, a soft, almost bluish green that reminded him of delicately carved jade statues. Whatever it was, he found it disturbing.

He moved beside her, smelled the wild scent of the storm she'd brought in with her, then reached down and pulled the photographs from her white knuckles. She looked at him, her eyes wide and questioning.

"I—I don't understand," she said quietly. "How... Who took these?"

Kane laid the pictures on the desk, then sat on the edge, blocking her view of them. "We don't know yet. The police are checking out what appears to be a thumbprint on the film case, but the film itself is standard and could be purchased at any one of a hundred stores in this area alone."

She straightened and her gaze darted to her father. "Has someone threatened you?"

Oliver shook his head. "Only by taking those pictures. But we weren't the only ones on that roll of film, Allison. There were two other people, local businessmen like myself, well known in the community. They both live on Fox Island within two or three blocks of our house, and they're both wealthy." His frown deepened. "And that was just one roll of film. There's no way of knowing how many more photographs this person—or persons—has taken."

The thought of someone following her, watching her, taking pictures... Allison tugged her skirt down over her knees. "What about the police?"

Oliver's sigh had a strong note of exasperation. "There's been no real threat, just some kook taking pictures. A kook we can't even identify," he added with annoyance.

Allison glanced at Kane, then back to her father. "Your security team is more than capable of handling perverted photographers, Dad. I don't understand why you've brought in Mr. Kane."

"It's just a precaution, Allie." Oliver smiled reassuringly. "I've got to go to Los Angeles for a few days and I'll feel better if Kane keeps an eye on things."

Allison knew her father well enough to know when he wasn't being completely honest. She shifted her gaze to Kane. Something told her that if she wanted a direct answer, with no sugarcoating, this was the man to ask.

"Mr. Kane, my father has spent my entire life sheltering and protecting me. I know him well enough to recognize when he's hiding something from me. I would appreciate it if you would tell me what it is he's worried about."

Kane glanced at Oliver, who sighed, then nodded. Kane looked back at Allison. "Kidnapping."

"Kidnapping?" She shook her head in disbelief. "Celebrities or politicians I could maybe understand, but as far as money, there are lots of people here in Seattle with a great deal more than us."

"What might be pocket change to you could look like a life's fortune to one of these guys." Kane picked up a Waterford paperweight on the desk and examined it. "They'll look for an easy mark. The simple fact that you don't think it could happen to you makes you that easy mark. In case you weren't aware of it, kidnapping has become quite fashionable."

Allison bristled at Kane's patronizing tone, but she couldn't argue with the truth of his words. Last year one of her father's business associates had barely escaped an attempt and then six months ago the newspapers had been filled with the story of the cable-television CEO abducted at gunpoint from his car. His wife had paid the ransom and he was found the next day. Dead.

"What makes you so sure it's a kidnapping threat?" she asked. "What about extortion, or someone's twisted attempt at blackmail or even just some crazy that likes to take pictures?"

Impatience shifted Kane's shoulders. "Not too many photographers steal cars to take pictures. There's nothing incriminating about the photographs to suggest blackmail, and there's been no contact for extortion money. If you're betting with your lives, always take the safe bet. If there's no kidnapping attempt, the only thing you've lost is money."

She narrowed a cool gaze at him. "And that's easily replaceable, right?"

"A hell of a lot more replaceable than that pretty little head of yours."

A sharp response was on the tip of Allison's tongue, but her father cut her off.

"Allison." Oliver folded his hands in what Allison knew to be his authoritative pose. "I'm going to be away for the next few days. Kane has ordered extra security at the house and I want you to move in there until we catch this guy."

She started to protest, but realized her father's request was not unreasonable. Besides, she slept there quite often, anyway, and she still had her bedroom upstairs. She let out a long sigh, then nodded. "All right, Dad. If it makes you feel better."

She saw the relief in her father's eyes that she'd agreed, then the hesitation. "And one more thing—" he paused briefly and cleared his throat "—I'm going to have to ask you to take off a few days from the center."

Take off a few days? Stunned, Allison stared at her father. He knew how much the center meant to her. The kids there were her life. She couldn't give that up, not even for a few days. Not for some creep with a camera. Not for anyone.

Shaking her head, she stood and moved behind her chair. "I can't do that, Dad. They're shorthanded right now and one of the boys, Billy, just came back from the hospital today following ear surgery. I promised him I'd be there in the morning to check up on him."

"Allison, please," Oliver said with such quiet desperation that she felt her determination slip. Her father always demanded or he asked, but he never pleaded.

"I've taken a lot of chances in my life," he continued, "and if it were just myself I wouldn't give this more than a second thought. But you're in those pictures, too. You're the one thing in my life I would never take chances with. Every time you go out in public you'll be exposing yourself to danger. Kane and I have already agreed that the best thing is for you to stay in the house—"

"*Kane* and you agreed?" Anger warmed the chill in the pit of her stomach, anger not only at the intrusion in her life, but that this man Kane, a man she'd never met, was already making decisions for her. Jaw tight, eyes narrowed, she turned to him.

"That's another thing I don't understand," she said stiffly, holding Kane's aloof gaze. "My father employs a reputable security company here at the pavilion, but I've never seen you before. Just exactly who are you?"

He stood slowly and moved toward her, stopping only inches away from her. He leaned close, close enough she could smell the masculine scent of his skin and see the subtle variations of deep blue in his eyes. A circle of tension surrounded her, then closed in, tighter and tighter, until she felt as if she could barely breathe. He gazed down intently.

"I'm the best, that's who."

He spoke with such conviction that only a fool would argue the point. His words were quiet, but he was a man who did not need to raise his voice to get attention, he simply needed to walk into a room.

And he definitely had her attention.

A knock at the office door sounded and Mrs. Harwood stuck her head in. "May I see you for a moment, Mr. Westcott?"

Nodding, Oliver stood. His concerned gaze held Allison. "I know this is a lot coming at you at once, Allison, but there's no other way to handle this."

"Dad—"

"Please, baby," Oliver said, brushing the hair back from her face, "just cooperate with Kane. I know he has some questions for you. I'll be back in a few minutes."

With a sigh, Allison folded her arms tightly and walked to the window. *Cooperate with Kane.* Cooperate wasn't the exact meaning here. More like obey. Frustrated, she drew in a slow, fortifying breath and watched a jagged bolt of lightning burst from the clouds.

"You okay?" Kane asked as he moved beside her.

She wasn't okay. But she sure wasn't going to let him know that. "My father said you have some questions."

He leaned against the windowsill, facing her. "Have you noticed anything unusual these last few days? Anything out of the ordinary?"

"No."

"Someone's following you and your father, Allison," Kane said sharply. "If you want me to find them before they find either one of you, then I need your help. I need you to think and think carefully. Have you seen anyone with a camera? The same car more than once? Has anyone stared at you, then quickly looked away?"

Kane watched Allison's brow furrow as she considered his question. He realized his last question was a stupid one. What man wouldn't stare at this woman? Or want to take her picture, for that matter? She was a photographer's dream: a long, sensuous neck, high cheekbones, thick, dark lashes surrounding expressive wide-set eyes. Eyes a man could drown in, if he wasn't careful. But Kane, of course, was always careful.

He stared at Allison's reflection in the window, watching her closely as she looked down at the streets below. There was something extraordinary about her, something fragile yet strong at the same time. He knew that she'd studied and taught ballet until she was twenty-four, and had danced professionally until she'd hurt her knee two years ago. She had the lean, slender body of a dancer, small, delicately rounded breasts and legs that would stop traffic.

Under different circumstances he would have pursued this woman with the same diligence he pursued everything in life. But the circumstances wouldn't allow it. He never became involved with clients, not even for a weekend, which was what he would have had in mind with Allison. He allowed himself one brief image of her stretched out naked beneath him, then quickly banished the thought before his body could react.

Damn. He nearly sighed out loud. It would have been a hell of a weekend.

She continued to stare out the window and her voice was distant when she spoke. "I've been spending a lot of extra time at work lately, and other than lunch with my father I haven't been anywhere."

"You were out to dinner three nights ago with a man named Michael Peterson."

Eyes wide, Allison turned and looked sharply at Kane. "So I was, Mr. Kane. And how would you happen to know that?"

He had her full attention now. Good. "What I know and how I know it isn't important. What *is* important is that you try to remember where you've been this last week, especially on the days those pictures were taken. Everywhere you went, everyone you talked to and everyone who talked to you. Think carefully."

Allison was having trouble thinking at all. First she'd had the shock of the pictures, and now this man was nonchalantly reporting who she'd been to dinner with. She was beginning to wonder who she should be more worried about—the man taking the pictures or Mr. Thomas Kane.

"I'd remember anyone strange at the center," she said with exasperation. "But beyond that I couldn't possibly remember every person I've talked to."

"You have to remember," he insisted. "A clerk, a waiter, someone who may have asked you for the time or held the door for you. Anything and everything. It might matter a lot to you, and to your father, as well."

Her father. She remembered the murdered CEO and closed her eyes, concentrating, forcing her mind to recall every movement of the last few days, to search for anything even remotely out of the ordinary.

There was the dry cleaners'…the service on her car… dinner with Michael…

Nothing exciting and certainly nothing out of the ordinary.

Sighing, she looked at Kane and shook her head. "I couldn't even tell you what I had for dinner the other night."

"Chicken amandine."

Stunned, she simply stared at him. And then something incredible happened.

He smiled.

Well, almost a smile, Allison corrected. It was more like the slightest uplifting of one corner of his mouth and an imperceptible tightening at the edges of his eyes. Though only for a second, the hard, sharp angles of his face softened. The change was subtle, but the effect was overwhelming. She felt the steady, deep thud of her heart and cursed herself for finding him attractive. "You mentioned my father hired you because you're the best, Mr. Kane. What exactly is it that you're best at?"

Too late, Allison realized the sexual nature of her question. In the briefest moment, as they stared at each other, it seemed as if the storm had moved into the room with them and charged the air with electricity. She felt it skipping up her back and tightening her skin. She held her breath, anticipating his answer.

"Kidnapping."

She blinked slowly. "You kidnap people?"

Kane's smile widened a fraction. "I'm more interested in prevention."

"That's what you do?" She lowered her brow. "You prevent kidnappings?"

"It's a living." A good one, Kane might have added, but didn't. His business had increased fifteen percent last year and he expected that figure to double this year. Men—and women—of wealth and power paid well to protect themselves and those they love. "My company is based in Miami. I have references, if you'd like to see them."

"That won't be necessary." This man needed no references, Allison thought. And it wasn't just his height or the muscular build of his body that was so formidable. There was a presence about him, a manner that radiated from him that was as primitive as it was powerful. A power that men respected and women responded to at the most basic level. And she, Allison noted with annoyance, was obviously no exception.

Reminding herself there was an issue here much more important than her own hormones waking up from hibernation, Allison stared down at the streets below. Cars were bumper to bumper in the rush-hour traffic. Windshield wipers swiped back and forth in syncopated rhythm. Thousands of people going home with nothing more on their minds than dinner with their families.

And somewhere down there was a man with a camera.

She turned slightly at the sound of men's voices from the outer office. "Those men in the hall, are they with you?"

"No." He stood beside her, following the movement of traffic. "They're part of your father's security team. I'm here to work with them, teach them what I know."

She wondered briefly who had taught Kane. "And what about our friend with the camera?" she asked quietly.

Kane would have liked to tell her that they'd catch the guy in a day or two and she could go about her business as usual. But he never made promises and he never underestimated a potential problem.

"He's already made a number of mistakes—stealing a car and losing the film for starters. My guess is that he'll make more. He's going to go after the wrong person, at the wrong time, and that's when we'll get him."

She turned to him, hugging her arms tightly to her. "And which 'wrong person' do you think he'll go after?"

He waited until her gaze lifted to his. "You."

Allison's eyes widened. "Well," she said on a shaky laugh, "you certainly don't mince words, do you?"

"Neither will a kidnapper."

She sucked in a sharp breath and nodded slowly. "So what now?"

"For now, it would certainly make life easier if you'd do as your father asks and stay home from work for a few days."

So they were back to that, Allison thought. She straightened her shoulders and leveled her gaze with Kane's. "Do you have any children?"

She could have sworn she saw him flinch, but then wondered if she'd imagined it.

"No."

"A wife?"

A hard glint entered his eyes. "No."

"Then it might be difficult for me to explain this to you, Mr. Kane, but I'm going to try anyway. There are twenty-five children at St. Martin's Center who look forward to seeing me. I take them to the movies, read to them, play games with them. All the things their drug-addicted or alcoholic mothers and fathers don't do."

Because she wanted him to understand, she leaned closer. "But there's something else I do that's even more important. I hold them. I kiss them. I tell them they're special, then wipe their tears away when they don't believe me. And then I hold them some more. For just a little while I share their pain, a pain that I thank God I never experienced, a pain that most people can't possibly understand.''

Kane let the old ache pass through him, ignoring the fact that it seemed sharper this time. Deeper. If he'd wanted to, he could have told her that he did understand. He understood too damn well. But he said nothing.

Allison clenched her hands into fists, angry not only at the situation, but at herself for trying to explain to this man why the center and the children there were so important to her. Based on the hard-set expression on his face, he hadn't heard a word she'd said. She wouldn't have believed it possible for one man to be so cold.

She told herself it didn't matter whether he understood or not, but that made it difficult to explain the profound sense of disappointment she suddenly felt. Needing to put some distance between herself and Kane, she turned away and walked back to her father's desk.

''I'm just going to say this one more time,'' she said quietly, but with resolution. ''I have no intention of hiding out while some jerk is on the loose. Those children need me, and even more I need them. We're practicing for a play right now, and I can't afford to be away. I'll stay at my father's house for as long as it's necessary, but that's as far as I compromise. I'll be going to the center every day except Tuesday, whether you like it or not.''

He didn't like it, but short of tying the woman up—and he admitted to himself the idea held interesting possibilities—there wasn't a hell of a lot he could do about it. It amazed him how quickly she'd shifted gears from fear to anger, and even though he decided he liked the way her green eyes lighted with determination, her insistence at keeping her regular schedule was going to make his life difficult. He sighed inwardly. It hardly would be the first time a woman had made his life difficult.

"Well, then, Miss Westcott—" he moved toward her, almost admiring the stubborn tilt of her chin as she held his gaze "—I guess we'll just have to manage, won't we?"

He felt her tense when he reached around her and picked up the photographs from the desk. He shuffled slowly through them, pausing at the picture of her in her underwear. Her bra was black and lacy, her matching panties a thin slip of fabric that one quick tug would easily remove. "But in the meantime, you might at least consider closing the blinds."

Allison understood that Kane was trying to intimidate her. And it was working, dammit. Heat rushed up her neck as she watched him stare at her picture. She pulled the photo from his fingers. "I'll do that."

The door opened and Oliver walked back into the office. A frown knotted his forehead. "I'm afraid I've got to leave now, Allison. I have a dinner meeting in Los Angeles tonight with one of our main buyers and I have a plane to catch." He picked up his briefcase under his desk, then gave Allison a kiss on the cheek.

She held onto his arm. "How can you leave right now? What if this guy is waiting for you?"

"I can't stop my life anymore than you can, sweetheart." Oliver took Allison's chin in his hand and met her concerned gaze. "I've got two men coming with me. I'll be home in a few days and we'll talk then. In the meantime, you'll be in good hands with Kane here."

Good hands with Kane? "But, Dad—"

"Sorry, hon'." He was already on his way out of the office. "Oh, and Allie—" he turned back around "—will you prepare the guest room for Kane? He'll be staying at the house with us."

Two

It was incredible how much one's life could change in a matter of a few minutes.

Allison stared at Kane's broad back, amazed at how smoothly he'd managed to maneuver her into the back corner of the crowded elevator and place himself between her and the rest of the people. The two men outside her father's office had also squeezed into the elevator, and they stood by the doors like guards at a palace gate.

She knew she should feel comforted by all the brawn surrounding her, but what she felt was smothered. She'd been on her own since she was eighteen—the year her mother had died—and she was used to coming and going as she liked, without an escort and certainly without asking permission. Having all these watchdogs around was going to take some getting used to. And in the case of Thomas Kane, she thought irritably, the adjustment was going to be a big one.

She stared at the wide stretch of shoulders blocking her view and cursed the warmth curling downward from her stomach. It was bad enough, this feeling of being on a leash, but the edge that Kane put her on was what disturbed her most of all. What was it about him, anyway? She'd certainly never been attracted to this type of man before. But then, she'd never met a man like Kane before. And the few men she had dated had been...what? *Ordinary,* was the word that came to mind. She frowned at the thought. What was wrong with ordinary? Absolutely nothing. They'd been nice, interesting men.

And they'd left her feeling tepid as tap water.

What made Kane so different? She casually lifted her chin and slid a glance at him, determined to find fault. He was too tall, she decided. Good Lord, he towered over her. She hated having to crane her neck to meet someone's eye. And he wasn't exactly *handsome,* at least, not in the classical sense, though there were certainly women who were attracted to his kind of rugged masculinity. The men she'd always been drawn to had been good-looking, the type of face you'd see in a men's fashion magazine. She stared at Kane's profile, thinking he looked more like an advertisement for a military-commando movie. It was easy to picture this man slashing his way through a steamy jungle, sweat dripping from his half-naked body....

Stop that. She jerked away her gaze and stared at the empty space over the head of the man standing beside Kane. What in the world was she doing, dreaming up silly fantasies about a man she'd met only minutes before? Didn't she have more important and certainly more serious things to think about? Things like some crazy following her, watching her, taking pictures...

The elevator stopped at the next floor, letting one person

off and two more on. The bustling forced Kane's body flush with hers. Embarrassment burned up her neck and over her cheeks as her breasts pressed into the solid muscle of his back. Her breath caught in her throat, her heart beat low and hard. Instinct had her raising her hands to force some distance between them, but logic had her drop them away again. Something very basic told her that to touch this man was a dangerous thing to do. And most annoying of all, she observed, was that Kane appeared completely oblivious to the intimate contact of their bodies. He seemed much more interested in the control panel over the elevator doors.

By the time the elevator finally reached the lobby, Allison wasn't sure her legs were sturdy enough to carry her out. She was almost thankful when Kane turned to her and took her by the arm.

"I'll need your keys."

"My keys?"

"Keys," he repeated, leading her across the lobby. "You know, what you use to open doors and start cars."

Frowning, she dug through her purse and pulled them out. "What do you—"

"Thanks." He took them from her as they walked outside. It had stopped raining and slivers of blue sky rimmed the once ominous clouds. When they reached her minivan, Kane opened the passenger door and held it for her. Fuming, she got into the car, noticing the almost imperceptible nod that Kane gave the two security men who were getting into a white sedan three parking spaces away.

"I *am* capable of driving my own car," she stated when he slid into the seat beside her and started the engine.

"Under normal circumstances, I'm sure that's true." He checked the side and rearview mirrors, then eased the van into traffic. "But what would you do if someone pulled up beside you, pointed a gun at you and told you to pull over?''

The idea of anyone pointing a gun at her made her stomach tighten. ''I—I don't know. How can anyone know what they'd do in a crisis?''

''You damn well better know.'' He made a sudden U-turn in the middle of the street and headed west toward her apartment. ''Your life may depend on it.''

She was still gripping the armrests from his unexpected turn. ''Okay.'' She thought for a moment. ''I'd step on the accelerator.''

''Wrong. You slam on the brakes.''

''*What?*''

''First lesson, Allison. Listen carefully.'' His eyes narrowed with intensity as he glanced at her. ''Be aggressive, hit fast, hit hard, then get the hell out.''

She stared at him in disbelief. ''You're actually serious. For God sake's, Kane, we're not talking about a military operation here.''

''And we're not talking about the fairy kingdom of never-never land either, princess.''

Gritting her teeth, she bit back the first response that came into her mind and went with the second. ''Don't call me 'princess.'''

''Stop acting like one.'' Kane checked his rearview mirror again, satisfied that the sedan was still behind him. ''You need to understand a few things. I don't own a pair of kid gloves and I'm not here to hold your hand.''

Hold her hand. Allison wound her fingers so tightly around the armrests that the fabric creaked. ''I think you better understand a few things yourself, *Mr.* Kane. I don't need or want you to hold my hand. I'm more than capable of taking care of myself.''

He slanted her a look and smiled. "Hold on to that thought. Lessons begin bright and early."

She had no idea what he was talking about, nor did she care to ask. Kane pulled up in front of her apartment a few minutes later and after she packed a bag and watered her house plants, they were back on the road again, crossing the bridge over the sound, heading toward Fox Island. They'd be at her father's house in about ten minutes and all she could think about was getting out of her heels, into a soft, comfortable pair of flats and her favorite sweatshirt.

To say that it had been a long day was putting it somewhat mildly.

"Oh, and one other thing," Kane said suddenly, breaking the long silence. "I'll need a list of men you've dated and/or slept with."

She hadn't heard him right. She couldn't have. He'd asked her for a list of lovers as casually as if he'd been asking her the time of day. She turned slowly in her seat and simply stared at him. "Excuse me?"

"I'll need a list of men you've—"

"Don't you dare say it again." Her jaw was clenched so tight she could barely speak. "Don't even think it. Whom I've dated, or as you so eloquently put it, 'slept with,' is nobody's business but mine."

She decided it was a good thing after all that Kane was driving. If she'd been behind the wheel right now she probably would have driven off the bridge.

"It's not uncommon for the victim to have known their abductor beforehand," Kane said. "Quite often, intimately."

Allison settled back in her seat. "I guarantee that whoever this creep is, it's no one I know or who knows me. Sorry, Kane, but I suggest you find a more willing subject

if you're looking for kicks, and while you're at it, you could
certainly use a more creative approach.''

He smiled then, a slow, confident smile that made Allison's insides churn. ''Princess, let me tell you something—
When I 'get my kicks' as you say, I'm very creative, and
the lady is always willing.''

She didn't doubt for a second what he said was true.
She'd already had a firsthand experience with the man's
appeal. Because she didn't want him to see her cheeks turn
red, she turned away and stared out the window. All she
could manage to say was, ''Don't call me 'princess.'''

This was not going to be easy.

Kane stood at the southwest edge of the cliffs behind the
Westcott estate and scanned an experienced eye over the
luxuriant grounds. Inside a five-foot brick wall surrounding
the property, flowering trees and perfectly manicured shrubs
nearly engulfed the two-story Spanish-style house. The
greenery was aesthetically pleasing, but a virtual haven for
uninvited guests, he thought with more than a twinge of
annoyance.

And the house had more windows than Seattle had rain.

One specific window on the second story—the bedroom
Allison slept in—drew his attention, and he mentally cal-
culated his position. Based on the angle of the shot, Kane
was sure this was the spot where their ''shutterbug'' had
been standing when he'd taken his picture. The rocks here
were big enough to easily hide behind and access from the
beach below was an easy climb. The spot was so remote
that it was doubtful any neighbor would have spotted him,
and even if Allison had seen him, she was so naive she
probably would have just waved at the guy. Hell, she probably would have invited him in for lunch.

He could still see the look on her face when she'd stared at the photograph of herself in her underwear. Her skin had paled against her dark hair and her fingers had felt like slivers of ice when he'd taken the picture out of her hands. He knew she was scared to death, he'd seen the fear in her wide eyes. Yet still she refused to spend the next few days here, inside, where she would be safer, out of danger.

Why, dammit? He shook his head irritably. What difference could it possibly make if she skipped a few days at the center and postponed the kids' show? So maybe the kids would be disappointed. Disappointment never killed a kid. If it did, he'd have been dead by the ripe old age of seven.

He turned sharply at the shriek of a sea gull overhead and watched the bird as it swooped low over the water. For some strange reason, the smooth motion of the creature made him think of Allison. She moved with that same powerful and elegant grace. And even though he knew that she'd studied ballet, hers was a grace that no amount of dance lessons could ever teach. It was completely natural, utterly feminine and disturbingly sensual.

He could still feel the soft pressure of her breasts on his back when they'd stood in the elevator this morning. The heat of her body had burned straight through his clothes and scorched his skin. Thirty seconds more with her pressed against him like that and he would have broken out in a sweat. He was going to have to be careful to keep his distance from her, he resolved. A woman like Allison could easily mess up a man's thinking, make him lose control. And control was something Kane had no intention of relinquishing.

He thought of the file he'd read on the plane this morning. Allison's file. She'd graduated from the dance academy six years ago, and the rest of her life had been as easy to read as a children's book, complete with pictures. Her career as a dancer had been notable, but her offstage life seemed to be virtually nonexistent. Though there'd been an occasional boyfriend mentioned in an entertainment magazine here and there, as far as he could see she'd had no serious affairs or rejected lovers.

He couldn't help the smile as he recalled the look of indignation on her face when he'd asked her about her personal life. He'd had to ask, that was his job, but any interest he might have in Allison's love life was purely professional. Unless one of those men was tied to the case, they had no relevance at all. They were simply nameless and faceless lovers who had no bearing on the current situation.

So why, then, was he trying to put a face to one of those men, wondering if he'd been another dancer she'd worked with, or maybe one of the dozens of admirers she must have had? What difference could it possibly make?

It didn't, he told himself. He was just getting restless. He'd worked nonstop for the last twelve months. There'd been little time for women, or any form of recreation, for that matter. As soon as this case was finished, he intended to find himself a long-legged blonde, a bottle of Jack Daniels and a quiet shack on an isolated beach in Bermuda.

He could see the ocean waves now, feel the warm breeze, a woman's long, slender legs wrapped around his bare body, her dark hair shining as it billowed out across the hot sand.

Dark hair? What happened to his blonde?

Damn. He rubbed a hand over his face. He needed this vacation sooner than he'd thought. In the meantime, he resolved, he'd better keep his mind on what Oliver Westcott was paying him to do, which was to keep his daughter safe.

Kane was comfortable with the competence of the men that had accompanied Oliver to Los Angeles and also with the three men who had been assigned to stay at the house on twenty-four-hour watch. Two of the men were to watch the outside perimeter and a third man was to tail Allison while she was en route from work and home. That was the trickiest part, keeping tabs on her once she left the estate.

He turned back to the house and stared at Allison's bedroom window again. His frown deepened. Why couldn't the woman understand she'd be better off here, in the safety of her own house? Any other woman would have run home and bolted the doors. Lord knew it certainly would have made his life a hell of a lot easier.

But then—Kane let out a long breath of exasperation— Allison Westcott was obviously not just any other woman. And she certainly was not going to make his life easier.

She came out of the house then and moved up the stone walkway toward him, with the ease of a woman who was comfortable with her surroundings. He watched as she approached, noting that she'd changed into a long oversize sweatshirt that matched the color of the pink azaleas along the path. Her pants—or whatever the modern fashion hounds called them—looked more like black tights than anything else, and while she certainly hadn't dressed to impress him, she looked so damn sexy that a jolt of desire shot through him before he had time to think.

He hoped like hell this job would be over soon.

"Thought you might like a cup of coffee." She stopped two feet away and handed him a steaming mug. "I hope black is all right."

Nodding gratefully, he accepted the cup, annoyed with himself that he'd intentionally avoided touching her hand. He watched as she combed her fingers through her hair, then folded her arms tightly in front of her. A nervous gesture. She moved to the edge of the cliff and stared silently at the approaching sunset.

"I noticed you were working with the alarm system this afternoon," she said finally, but did not turn to look at him.

"Just checking it out."

As she turned back to him, the ocean breeze tugged at the wild mass of curls around her face. He watched in fascination as her hand swept the hair away from her cheek.

"And?"

He'd never been one to soften the truth before, and he didn't intend to start now. "Before I ordered a few adjustments, I doubt it would have kept out the Avon lady."

She winced, then recovered quickly. "And now?"

He shrugged. "Now we probably only have to worry about insurance salesmen."

So the man does have a sense of humor, Allison thought with mild surprise. She felt the tightness in her shoulders ease, as she realized that if anyone did try to break in, they not only had to get through the two men stationed outside and Kane's updated alarm system, but they had to get through Kane himself. Something told her that was not an easy thing to do. "So what happens now?"

He wished she would stop chewing on her bottom lip. Though he knew she didn't intend the gesture to be provocative, that didn't make it any less so. He took a sip of his coffee, glad that it was as hot as it was strong. "Ideally, we find the guy before he makes a move."

"And if we don't find him?"

The waves lapped on the beach below and the distant sound of a speedboat hummed in the moist salt air. Kane was well aware of the fact that an approach to the Westcott estate from the water was a strong possibility. He watched the boat until it looped away. "Either way, we're ready for him."

She hugged her arms tightly around her. "We moved into this house when I was ten. I played on the beach all day and at night, as well. I never once felt there was any danger." She sighed and stared back at the house. "It's so strange, not feeling safe here, not knowing whom to trust."

"That's the easy part." His eyes narrowed as he lifted his cup to his mouth again. "Don't trust anyone."

"What about you, Kane?" She glanced back at him. "Am I supposed to trust you?"

His jaw tightened. "I'm here to do a job. That you can depend on. Nothing more, nothing less."

She sent him an exasperated look. "Has anyone ever told you it's not healthy to go around suspecting everyone?"

"It's not healthy to be dead, either."

Allison felt the impact of Kane's words like a punch in the stomach. He never let up, not even for a second, and she wondered if some sadistic part of him enjoyed keeping her on the edge. "Thanks for the reassurance. I'm sure that little bit of advice will help me sleep much better tonight."

She started to walk away then, but he caught her by the wrist.

"Allison."

She wasn't sure what surprised her more, the gentle touch of his hand or the uncharacteristic softness in his voice. She stared at his fingers wrapped around her wrist, then lifted her eyes to his. For a brief second, a flash of something—tenderness?—was there in his eyes, but it was gone so quickly she might have imagined it.

"I'm not here so you can sleep better at night," he said quietly. "You can't let your guard down, not even for a minute. My job is to keep whoever this guy is out there from getting close to you. Your job is to be ready and prepared for anything. You'll get no kind words from me, no assurances, because there are none. That's how I operate and that's why your father hired me.''

She was beginning to understand more clearly why her father *had* hired Kane. The two men were very much alike. As subtle as a steamroller and as tenacious as an angry bull. Results were what mattered, not merit badges in charm. She may not like it, but she did respect it.

As he let go of her arm she realized that he'd come about as close to an apology or explanation as she'd ever get from him. Though unspoken, a truce settled between them. ''Dinner's in the oven, but it won't be ready for about forty-five minutes.''

Kane remembered that he'd already spoken to the gardener and the pool man, but he hadn't seen a glimpse of the housekeeper and cook that Oliver employed full-time. ''I'll need a few minutes of your housekeeper's time after dinner. I need to ask her a few questions.''

''That might be a little difficult,'' Allison said, feeling a twinge of satisfaction that there were a few things Mr. Thomas Kane didn't know. ''Her granddaughter just had a baby yesterday. She left this morning to stay with her for a month.''

Confused, Kane glanced toward the house. ''Who's cooking?''

Good Lord, did the man think she was entirely helpless? She tapped down the annoyance rising in her. ''I've learned to throw one or two simple meals together.''

''I don't expect you to cook for me.'' Actually, he hadn't expected her to cook at all. The fact that she did surprised him.

Something told her that Kane never expected anything

from anybody. If a person didn't expect anything, then he didn't have to give anything. "There's plenty," she said flatly. "I've already asked the other men to join us."

Kane resisted the urge to roll his eyes. Next thing he knew, they'd be having a picnic. "I'll take a plate out to them," he said dryly. "These men are here to work, not attend dinner parties."

"Oh, darn." She gestured dramatically and sarcasm dripped off her words. "Now whoever will I wear my gown and jewels for tonight?"

He could see diamonds on her. Diamonds and emeralds and black velvet. "You'll be wearing them for our picture-taking friend, if you don't let us do our job."

Kane's words cooled Allison's ire and sharply reminded her of the situation. The idea of someone actually coming into her home while she was sleeping or taking a shower made her skin crawl. Having worked with the children at the center, she'd always thought she had a strong understanding of the darker side of life. But the truth was, she'd never been a victim herself. No one had ever threatened to hurt her; no one had ever followed her or watched her.

Or taken her picture while she was getting dressed.

Maybe Kane was right. Maybe she had been living in never-never land. Maybe 'princess' wasn't so far off, after all.

"I've got to go check on my frozen dinners," she said with just enough bite to lift her spirits a notch. "Those aluminum containers are awful to clean when you burn the macaroni and cheese."

Kane watched her walk away and wondered why he felt as if he'd just kicked a puppy. So what if she was mad at him? That was his intention. Anger kept people on their toes. And Allison needed to be alert. He had to remind her there were bad guys out there, no matter how angry it made her; no matter how much it upset her. It was for her own good, dammit.

He almost smiled as she disappeared into the house, realizing that however angry she might happen to be at him now, it was nothing compared to what she'd be feeling after she found out what he had planned for the morning.

Three

Barefoot, dressed in a leotard and tights, Allison tiptoed out of her bedroom and down the stairs, then quietly moved toward the back of the house. The chilly air brought goose bumps to her bare arms, but she welcomed the cold. Anything that would help her wake up at the ungodly hour of five-thirty in the morning was appreciated.

A small price to pay for privacy, she reminded herself, holding her breath as she paused outside the guest bedroom Kane was sleeping in. She leaned her head toward the door and listened. Absolute silence.

Smiling, she crept down the hallway, pleased that she'd found a few quiet moments for herself. Everywhere she'd turned last night, it had seemed as if Kane was there. Not that he'd stood over her shoulder or followed her around. If anything, it had been the opposite. He'd kept to himself most of the evening in the kitchen, studying maps and files, going outside periodically to talk with the other men. He'd barely acknowledged her the entire night.

And yet, though she'd hardly seen him, she still felt his presence. It didn't matter that he was in the other room or outside. There was an energy that pulsated through the house, a force that had never been there before. She realized, of course, that the situation itself called for a heightened sense of awareness on her part. After all, *someone* was out there, and whoever it was, he was watching her and her father.

But at a deeper level Allison knew that her anxiety, her apprehension, hadn't nearly as much to do with the circumstances as it did with Kane himself. Danger and excitement were inherent in the man, a part of who he was. His passion. She knew it, felt it instinctively, and as surely as it frightened her on one level, it seduced her on another.

And that, Allison told herself, was what made Thomas Kane such a dangerous man. A man to avoid at all costs. Even if it meant rising with the sun.

When she opened the door of the rec room, what she saw took her breath away.

He was there at the weight machine, his hands tightly clasped around the T-bar over his head, his arms rhythmically moving up and down, the movement as fluid as the sweat that glistened on his face and bare arms. He wore sweatpants and a ragged gray sweatshirt cut off at the shoulders. The underarms and chest were also stained from the exertion of his workout.

She should have left, simply backed out before he caught her staring at him, but her legs suddenly felt as heavy as the weights he lifted, her feet rooted to the cold wooden floor. She couldn't have looked away if she'd wanted to.

He was magnificent. His eyes were closed with intense

concentration; his jaw set hard as concrete. The muscles on his arms bunched and rippled under the force as he moved. He strained at the weights, teeth gritted, obviously pushing himself to and then beyond his limits. She watched in fascination, admiring not only the physical body, but the dedication, as well. She recognized the look on his face, the driving need to be the best. She'd seen it in more than one dancer's eyes and had even paid the price herself. Performances with pulled tendons. Practices with wrapped, bleeding toes. Dancing was all she'd ever known, all she'd ever wanted, and when she'd had her accident she'd thought it a curse. But now, when she looked into the faces of her children at the center, she knew in her heart it had been a blessing.

The weights clattered down, startling her. Her gaze met his and they stared at each other, neither one of them moving. The silence of the room closed around them, held them. She heard the sound of her own heartbeat, felt her body tighten like the string of a violin, waiting for the pull of the bow....

When he looked away and reached for a towel on the weight bench, she breathed a silent sigh of relief.

"I'm sorry." She started to back out. "I'll come back later."

Breathing hard, he waved her back into the room as he wiped at the sweat on his face and neck. "You're early." He gasped between breaths.

The rapid rise and fall of his chest held her attention. Sweat rimmed the top of his sweatshirt. She pulled her gaze from his body. "What do you mean, 'I'm early?'"

He glanced at the clock on the mirrored wall behind Allison. "You don't work out until six-thirty."

Was there anything this man didn't know about her?

Frowning, she stepped into the room. "And where did you happen to get that little bit of information?"

"Your father mentioned it." He dragged the towel over his damp hair, then wrapped it around his neck.

"After you asked, you mean."

He reached for the thermos beside the weight machine, twisted the top off and poured the steaming liquid into the cup. "Coffee?"

No sane person turned down coffee at this hour of the morning. She took the plastic cup out of his hand, hoping that something hot would steady her shaky nerves. "Just a swallow," she said, taking a sip.

"Go ahead and finish it." He stood and tossed the towel over the weight bench. "The extra caffeine will do you good before we start."

She eyed him suspiciously. "What do you mean 'before we start?'"

"Your lessons."

"What *lessons?*"

He shook his arms out, then planted himself in front of her, his feet spread slightly apart. "I'm going to teach you self-defense."

Self-defense? Allison lowered the cup and stared at him incredulously. "You mean like karate or judo?"

"Not exactly. I'll just work with you on some simple but effective techniques to protect yourself."

The coffee obviously wasn't helping her nerves at all. She tightened her fingers around the cup, struggling to hold on to her composure. "I thought it was *your* job to protect me."

"And what if I can't?" He stared down at her. "What if these guys manage to get you alone, or what if I'm shot or even dead. There'll be no one but you, Allison. Then what?''

The thought of Kane being hurt while he was protecting her horrified Allison. And the idea of violence, even in her own self-defense, made her stomach twist painfully. ''I don't know.''

''You *have* to know. You either take responsibility for yourself or you'll be a victim, no different from your kids at the center.''

The anger that shot through her was as swift as it was furious. She leveled her gaze with his, and the fact that he was a good nine inches taller was irrelevant. ''You leave the children out of this. They have no choice in their lives.''

He nodded stiffly. ''That's right. They had no choice at all. But you do. You can walk out of here, or you can be a headline in the morning newspapers whom everyone feels sorry for. What'll it be?''

She wanted to walk away, *needed* to walk away. But the truth of Kane's words permeated the fist of anger gripping her. He was right. She did have a choice.

Setting her jaw, she drew in a slow, deep breath and handed him the cup back. ''Just get on with it.''

Kane took the cup from Allison's hand, watching her eyes shift from the hard edge of anger to the rigid set of determination. Good. Tenacity was always the best pupil, not size or gender. He forced himself to hold her gaze, refusing to give in to the impulse to skim over the curves beneath the skintight outfit she wore that—much to his discomfort—more than defined her gender and size.

Setting the cup behind him, he faced her again. ''The first rule, and most important, is to be aware of what's happening around you. Watch the movements of anyone walking close by. Keep track of the traffic around you. Always know what your options are, what street you can pull onto, where you can run for help. Be alert to anything, or anybody, out of the ordinary.''

"Someone like you, maybe?'' Sarcasm edged her words.

One corner of his mouth tipped upward. "Especially someone like me.''

He moved closer to her and Allison realized he was intentionally trying to intimidate her. Though the impulse to step back was strong, she held her ground, trying to ignore the rapid-fire beating of her heart. "And what if I can't get away?''

He moved closer still. "That's when you need to keep calm and assess the situation. Does he have a gun? A knife? What's close to you that you might use as a weapon yourself? Your keys, your purse, a picture frame or rolled-up magazine. Anything you can strike with quickly, that will give you the extra seconds you need to run.''

What she wanted to do was run out of here. *Dammit.* He was too close. The clothes he'd been wearing yesterday hadn't revealed how *muscular* he was. His arms were like cords of steel, his chest as wide as a doorway. She knew that fact should make her feel safe, but at the moment she felt anything but.

"Most assailants,'' he went on, "expect pleading and acquiescence, not a counterattack. Use that to your advantage. Beg with them not to hurt you, then let them have it while they're gloating over their dominance.''

"Hit hard, hit fast and get the hell out,'' she quoted Kane from yesterday.

"Good girl.'' He smiled. "You pay attention.''

She wondered if he had any idea just how true his statement was. With no more than ten inches between them, he *definitely* had her undivided attention. The masculine scent of his skin, the waves of heat radiating off his body. And his eyes. His eyes were deep blue, as brilliant and endless as a moonlit sky.

Dealing with an attack was beginning to look like a piece of cake next to dealing with Kane.

Her hands curled into fists at her sides. "Now what?"

"Now—" he grabbed her suddenly "—you're going to learn how to take the offensive."

With his hands wrapped tightly around Allison's wrists, Kane wasn't sure who was surprised more—Allison or himself. He'd intended to catch her off guard, of course, but he certainly hadn't planned to be caught as well.

Her skin was cool and soft beneath his hands, her scent distinctly feminine. As he stared down at her wide green eyes and softly parted lips, he had to remind himself—again—that Allison Westcott was a client. A beautiful one perhaps, but a client nonetheless. When she tried to pull away from him he held fast.

She narrowed her eyes. "You really expect me to be able to break out of your hold?"

"Every hold has a weak point. Mine is here—" he lifted her arms "—between my thumb and forefinger. Twist your arms," he instructed, "then quickly pull down and away."

He had to be kidding, she thought. His hands were like twin bands of iron on her arms. Still, she did as he said. And all she managed to achieve was two sore wrists. She glared at him. "Kane, I can't—"

"Just think of it as a dance movement," he encouraged. "Fast and furious, yet smooth and even. Concentrate. Focus on that weak point and pull your own strength from deep inside."

"I can't—"

He drew her closer to him. "I'm not giving you a choice.

You either break out, or we'll be standing here all day.'' One corner of his mouth tipped upward. ''Just you and me, Allison. Alone.''

The suggestive tone in Kane's voice was all the incentive Allison needed. Jaw set, shoulders straight, she twisted her arms, pulled down and away.

It worked.

She stared at her free arms. *She'd done it.* She'd actually broken out of his hold. Amazed, she looked at Kane. He grinned at her with that damn I-told-you-so look. The temptation to frown at him was strong, but the satisfaction that rippled through her wouldn't let her. Instead, she smiled slowly and put her hands on her hips. ''All right, Mr. Kane,'' she said as she faced him. ''You've got me for one hour before I have to get ready for work. Teach me what you know.''

Two hours later, sitting next to Kane on the drive into Seattle, Allison was already regretting those words.

One hour with Kane had left her feeling as if she'd been run over by a herd of elephants. It was putting it mildly to say that the lesson—like the man himself—had been intense. Her arms were sore from being grabbed and twisted, her wrists bruised and her weak knee, sensitive to extreme movement, was throbbing from the kicks he'd taught her.

But the physical discomfort was nothing compared to the emotional turmoil she was feeling. Though Kane had been completely professional, aloof even, the feel of his hands on her, his body pressed against hers repeatedly, had left her a nervous wreck. The contact might not have been gentle, but it sure as hell had been intimate, and her reaction to his closeness was anything but professional.

And Kane hadn't batted an eye, not even when he'd

wrapped his arms tightly around her and held her against him while he instructed her on the move to break out. It had taken every ounce of mind power to even listen to him, let alone follow his directions. She'd failed miserably on that hold, which only meant that they had to practice it more than all the others. Over and over he'd held her, and each time it seemed closer and tighter, until she felt as if he might pull her inside him.

Frowning, she glanced over at him. Not once, not when he'd held her, not even when her breasts had been crushed against his chest, had she seen his expression change. Not once had he looked at her as a man looks at a woman.

So what if she wasn't his type? she thought irritably. It certainly shouldn't bother her because one man was indifferent to her.

She settled back into her seat and stared out the window. So why then, did she feel so damn annoyed?

When it started to rain again, Kane began to seriously wonder if Seattle ever saw blue sky. It was certainly a far cry from Florida. Swearing silently, he flipped on the windshield wipers and checked the rearview mirror for the white sedan that had been with them since they'd left the house. The sedan, driven by a kid named Tony Salinas, was two car lengths behind. Tony had only worked security for Oliver Westcott for the past six months, and at twenty-five he hadn't the experience Kane would have preferred. But his records were clean and the six years he'd spent in the navy had earned him a congressional Medal of Honor following a skirmish in the Gulf. Though Kane had little respect left for the military itself, he had tremendous respect for the men who enlisted and served. When Kane exited the freeway, Tony followed.

Beside him, Allison gestured to the left. "Take the next turn at—"

"Second Street," he finished for her.

She frowned at him, then glanced back at the car following them. "I still don't understand why it's necessary for both you and Tony to come to the center with me. There's at least a dozen people around all the time. What could possibly happen?"

He looked at her sharply. "How well do you know Tony?"

"Tony Salinas?"

"How well?" Impatience edged his words.

She definitely didn't like the implication she heard in Kane's voice. "Not well at all," she ground out.

The back wheels of the van skidded as Kane took the turn too fast. "I told you I'm not interested in your personal life, Allison. I'm just doing my job. If Tony's objectivity might be blurred because you two have—or had—something going, I'll request someone else."

She faced him, carefully enunciating her words. "I do not have—nor have I ever had—a relationship with Tony Salinas. I've met him exactly twice, both times in a professional capacity as security for my father's company."

Arms folded tightly, she turned away. Kane might have smiled at her irritation, but the fact was he was feeling the same damn thing. He tried to tell himself it was the lack of clues and suspects he had to work with on this case, but he knew—whether he wanted to admit it or not—that wasn't the truth.

It was Allison.

He'd always been a man who liked living on the edge. He thrived on it. The constant sense of danger, of excitement, was as essential to him as breathing. But when a woman was involved, the edge was too dangerous, even for him. And that's how Allison made him feel. On edge.

She'd done well this morning, he conceded. Better than he'd expected, especially considering the paces he'd put her through. A crash course in self-defense was not a simple task. He hadn't gone easy on her and he hadn't been gentle. There was no time. They went through the moves over and over, and they'd go over and over them again tomorrow and the day after that and every day until she knew them backward, forward and in her sleep. Until she learned to react to a threat sharply and instinctively.

He looked at her, followed the movement of her long, slender fingers as she pulled on the collar of the pink silk blouse she had on. His hands tightened on the steering wheel. He'd touched her no more than an hour ago and the image of her skin, as soft and smooth as the silk she wore, lingered with him. He had a sudden unwanted urge to touch her again, an urge that had nothing to do with self-defense and everything to do with plain old-fashioned lust. He wanted to slowly unbutton her blouse and slide it over her shoulders, then run his hands over the swell of her breasts and—

"You missed your turn."

He glanced over at her. "What?"

Chin raised slightly, she turned to him. "You just drove by the center."

He made a left turn at the next street. "We're going to come up behind it." He turned left again. "If anyone's watching, they'll expect you to drive up the same way you always do. I intend to make life difficult for them every place I can."

Not nearly as difficult as he was making her life, Allison thought. She looked over at him, watching as he pulled into

the back parking lot of the center. He kept his emotions—
if he had any—contained. He was two steps ahead of everyone else, ready for anything. In control.

Sighing inwardly, she picked up her purse as Kane slid
into a parking spot. She was going to have to get tough,
she told herself. That was the only effective counterattack
to a man like Kane.

The center was already alive with sound when Allison
walked through the back doors with Kane at her side. The
shrill of children talking and laughing, the clatter of silver-
ware against plates, the drone of a distant TV. It was one
of the things that drew her here day after day: the energy
that pulsated through every room and echoed in the halls.
She turned to Kane. ''They're having breakfast now, we
can—''

''Allison!''

The screech startled Kane and he tensed, then relaxed as
a child—a little girl around five or six with hair the color
of corn silk—flung herself at Allison's legs and hung on.
Children were an oddity to Kane. He'd never had any, nor
had he ever been around them. He watched, fascinated yet
strangely awkward, as Allison hoisted the child up and spun
her. It was the first time Kane had heard Allison laugh, and
the sound rippled through him like warm velvet.

''Good morning, Courtney.'' Allison kissed the five-
year-old's rosy cheek. ''Why aren't you eating breakfast?''

''I was waiting for you.'' Courtney spotted Kane at that
moment and quickly hid her face in Allison's neck.

''This is my friend, Kane,'' Allison said gently to the
child. ''He's going to be visiting with us for a few days. Is
that all right?''

Courtney seemed to burrow deeper into Allison's neck
and shook her head.

"He's a very nice man." Frowning, Allison looked at Kane and waved her hand, encouraging him to say something.

Dumbstruck, Kane simply stared at Allison and the youngster. He'd met prime ministers, dignitaries, movie stars—even the president of the United States—and he'd never been at a loss for words. All of a sudden, one little girl had him tongue-tied and brain-dead. Allison's frown deepened.

"Ah," he muttered, struggling for words, "that's a pretty lace ruffle on your dress, Courtney."

Kane groaned inwardly. What a stupid thing to say. He decided he'd rather dismantle a land mine than make conversation with a child.

Courtney stole a peek at Kane and smiled. Amazed, Kane met Allison's gaze. Damned if she wasn't smiling, too.

"You go ahead and eat now, sweetie." Allison set the little girl down. "I'll be there in a minute, after I say good morning to Billy."

The child's tennis shoes squeaked on the green tile floor as she scampered off. Allison looked at Kane, one brow raised in approval. "I wouldn't have thought you were a man who noticed lace ruffles on little girls."

His smile was slow but deliberate. "I've never been around little girls, but on big girls lace always attracts my attention." He leaned close and put a finger on her shoulder. "Silk is nice, too."

A jolt went through Allison at Kane's touch. He ran his finger down her arm, and for one brief moment she could have sworn she saw the flare of desire in his dark eyes. But it was gone as quickly as it appeared, and when he dropped his hand away his face was as shuttered as a house in a hurricane.

Her legs were unsteady as she turned from him and when she paused at the dining-room doorway to wave hello to the children and staff having breakfast, their boisterous greeting was a welcome distraction. She hurried down the hall, anxious not only to see Billy but to put some distance between herself and Kane.

Kane followed several feet behind, angry with himself for letting his control slip. One simple touch and he'd ached to pull Allison into his arms, to feel her nestled as securely against him as she'd held Courtney. *Damn.* He was losing it—something he couldn't afford to do. He was going to have to be careful, very careful, when it came to this woman.

He watched her walk down the hall, stopping at one door to say hello to a child in bed with the chicken pox. She was in her element here, he acknowledged. The kids obviously loved her, and based on the light in her eyes as she'd held Courtney and waved good morning to the kids in the dining room, she loved them, too.

When she disappeared into a room at the end of the hall, he stopped at the doorway. Inside the room, a dark-haired boy around eight or nine was sitting up in his bed watching a small black-and-white TV on the nightstand.

"Hi, Billy." Allison sat on the bed beside the boy. "How's your ear feeling today?"

Billy continued to stare at the TV. "Okay."

"Billy, this is Kane, a friend of mine." She turned toward the doorway. "He'll be visiting with us for a few days."

The child looked sullenly at Kane, then turned his attention back to the game show he was watching.

"Okay if I turn that off?" She gestured toward the TV. The child shrugged. "Picture's no good anyhow."

She turned off the set, then reached into her purse and pulled out something that looked like a remote control. "I thought maybe you could help me out. Someone gave this to me and I don't know what to do with it."

Though dim, a light sparked in Billy's eyes. "That's a Game Mania."

"I'm not very good at buttons and mechanics." She pushed a button and electronic music signaled the start of a game. "Maybe you could figure out how to work this thing then show me?"

"Sure." A smile tilted Billy's lips as he reached for the game. The smile suddenly faded as he stared at Allison's hand.

Puzzled by the change in Billy's expression, Allison followed his gaze and realized what had caught the child's attention.

There were bruises on her wrist.

"Billy," she said gently, "it's okay. Kane was teaching me some neat karate moves." She looked back at Kane, who leaned against the doorjamb, then nearly laughed at the unexpected look of guilt on his face. "Maybe when you feel better, he can teach you some, too. Would you like that?"

Billy stared at Kane suspiciously, but nodded slowly.

"Good morning, everyone."

Allison turned and saw Suzanne Smith standing at the doorway with a breakfast tray. Suzanne, a drop-dead-gorgeous blonde, had been with the center for almost a year, and her soft Southern manner had won everyone over. Based on the look Kane was giving her, Allison thought irritably, Suzanne was about to make another conquest.

"Am I missing something?" Suzanne asked, stepping past Kane into the room.

Teeth gritted, Allison introduced Kane to the woman, but gave no explanations why he was here. *Let her wonder for a while.*

Patting Billy's leg, Allison stood. "I'll be back later for my first Game Mania lesson. Think you can handle it?"

Nodding, the child clutched the game tightly, and the smile he gave Allison brought a tightness to her chest. She moved to the door, stiffening as she walked past Kane.

"Hey."

She was halfway down the hall when he called to her. Ignoring him, she turned left down another hallway and headed for the arts-and-crafts room.

"Dammit, Allison, hold up." He caught her arm and held her still.

Eyes narrowed, she leveled a gaze at him that could have melted steel. "No swearing inside these walls, and absolutely nothing that even remotely resembles physical force."

Properly chastised, Kane dropped his hand. "What's eating you?"

She was hardly about to tell him that she was perturbed because he'd looked at Suzanne but hadn't given her so much as a second glance. It was silly and childish and completely unreasonable. Not to mention humiliating.

"I've got work to do. I don't interfere with your job. I expect the same consideration."

"What's Billy's story?"

That's what he'd stopped her for? To ask about Billy? She looked at him and saw genuine concern in his eyes. Sighing, she moved into the arts-and-crafts room then closed the door behind Kane when he stepped inside.

"His mother's boyfriend abused him for six months before an astute teacher became suspicious and questioned the mother,'' she said quietly. ''Afraid of charges being drawn up against them, the mother and the boyfriend took off, leaving Billy behind.''

Allison struggled to keep her voice even, to simply relate the facts as she knew them and keep her emotions at bay. The anger and heartache would consume her if she didn't. ''He was alone for three days. He fed himself and even went to school on his own. Finally a neighbor caught on and called the police. No one knows who the father is, and with no other family he'll stay here while he recovers from ear surgery and then he'll be placed in a foster home.''

''What about adoption?''

She shook her head. ''At his age, it's very rare.''

Jaw tight, Kane looked away, staring blindly at a pile of yellow construction paper cut into flowers. ''And Courtney?''

Allison took in a breath. ''Her mother and father are drug addicts. They're in rehab right now. The court will decide whether she'll be placed in a foster home or go back with them.''

Kane's face hardened. ''They'd let her go back to parents like that?''

''I can't think about that.'' Allison closed her eyes. ''The luck of the draw wasn't with these children when parents were passed out. I have no control other than to give them as much love and attention as I can while they're here.''

He stared at her, feeling a strange ache in his chest. He'd been wrong about her. She wasn't a rich prima donna volunteering a few hours because she had nothing else to do. She was as serious about her work as she was dedicated.

''Maybe they aren't completely unlucky, after all,'' he said quietly, reaching up to run his thumb over her cheek. ''They have you.''

The unexpected tenderness in Kane's touch and words nearly crumpled the last of Allison's composure. But she refused to let him see her cry. She'd vowed to get tough when it came to Kane and she intended to keep that vow.

Pulling away from him, she turned and busied herself collecting bright strips of fabric for the morning's art project.

And Kane sat back, watching, feeling as helpless as if he'd been caught on a fisherman's line that was being slowly and steadily reeled in.

Four

The noise woke Kane at 1:34 in the morning. It was barely more than a soft creak, a sound that could be as simple as the house settling or maybe even the scrape of a branch against a window. He sat, his ears strained, his body tense, listening....

Dead silence.

And still, though he heard nothing, he knew without a doubt that someone was in the house.

Too many years of listening in the dark had developed a sixth sense in Kane. He knew that silence could be just as deadly as the click of a gun's hammer or the quiet swish of a knife. Danger had a life of its own, an energy that hung in the air, invisible yet tangible. It was not to be ignored and it was certainly not to be dismissed.

He slid out of bed and reached for the automatic on his nightstand. Barefoot, dressed only in a pair of sweatpants, he opened the bedroom door and slipped into the darkness of the hall. He crouched low and pressed against the cool wall, waiting…waiting….

There it was again. Barely audible. A soft click. It came from the end of the hall, from the garage….

His fingers tightened on the gun's handle and, catlike, he moved toward the sound, staying close to the wall. He thought briefly of Allison, sleeping upstairs, and hoped like hell she'd kept her door locked as he'd instructed.

The hallway was pitch-black, except for the soft green glow of the alarm panel beside the door leading into the garage. Kane's stomach knotted as he stared at the panel. He'd activated the alarm when he'd gone to bed and the red light had been on. Now, there was no red light.

Someone had shut off the alarm system.

Jaw tight, breath held, Kane stepped into the dark garage. The concrete was cold and smooth beneath his feet. A pencil-thin strip of light flashed suddenly from the back seat of Allison's van, then disappeared.

Dammit! How had someone slipped past the men outside? Soundlessly, Kane moved around the back of the van. It was too dark to make out a shape, but what looked like a leg protruded from the open door of the back seat. When the leg jerked upward, Kane swung into position and raised his gun.

"You so much as move a toe and you're a dead man."

The figure went absolutely still. "That would be interesting," an obviously feminine voice replied.

Allison! Kane drew in a deep breath, waiting for the rush of adrenaline to pass. Anger quickly took its place.

"What the hell are you doing out here?" He laid his gun on the roof of the van.

There was a tense silence, then, "I'm stuck."

He knew he should turn on the overhead light in the van, but he didn't. For reasons he didn't want to examine, he preferred the darkness. Crawling into the van, he realized she was stretched across the back seat, lying on her side. "What do you mean, you're stuck?"

"My robe." She reached behind her, trying to unfasten herself. "I'm caught on something, but I can't see what."

Kane bent down on his knees beside her. "So why don't you take it off?"

A long pause emphasized the quiet. "I can't."

An awareness hung between them, a sudden understanding not only of the situation but of each other: she wasn't wearing anything beneath the robe.

His throat went dry. The darkness tightened around him and he heard his pulse pounding in his ears. She was so close. So damn close. The intoxicating scent of her skin drifted to him and an ache spread through his body, a desperate need to touch her.

When he reached for her she didn't move, but her breathing deepened. He touched her arm, felt the warmth of her body through the thin robe. The cotton fabric was soft and smooth beneath his hand. Slowly he slid his hand down her back, pulling her away from the seat, closer to him. The robe pulled away from her shoulders, holding fast to the seat-belt buckle.

"Your belt loop is caught on the seat belt," he murmured, working his fingers to loosen the fabric.

"Oh," was all Allison could manage. Her heart was pounding so hard she was sure that Kane could not only hear it but feel it, as well. He'd wrapped one arm around her and his bare chest was no more than an inch from hers. Her breasts felt fuller, her skin tighter. Heat radiated off Kane's body and shimmered through her. His fingers worked blindly at her waist, pulling her steadily closer to him. She might have suggested he turn the light on, but she didn't.

"You never told me what you were doing out here."

The coarse texture of Kane's voice only increased the tension building in Allison. She forced herself to focus on his question, rather than the feel of his hands on her. "Courtney made me a rag doll today—yesterday," she corrected, realizing the time. "I realized I'd left it in the car and since I was having trouble sleeping anyway, I came down to find it."

Allison's breathless whisper only increased Kane's discomfort. When her breasts lightly brushed against his chest, he felt her hardened nipples and nearly groaned out loud. "Why didn't you turn on a light?"

She put her hand on his chest, trying to hold herself away from him, but her fingers on his hot skin sent the heat swirling low and fast in her stomach. "I...didn't want to wake you. I brought a penlight, figuring it would just take a second. Somehow, I ended up getting caught."

He was the one who was caught. She'd aroused him to the point of pain and the way her robe was opening in the front was only increasing his discomfort. When she touched him, his control snapped.

"The hell with it," he growled and ripped the loop loose.

Allison gasped as she fell against him. His arm was still around her, his lips a whisper away from hers. She felt the warm rush of his breath against her cheek. Neither one of them moved and the tension closed around them like a fist.

"Did you find it?" he asked quietly.

"Find it?"

His hand tightened on her waist. "The doll."

"Oh, yes. It...was under the back seat."

Her upper body was flush with his now, her breasts against his chest, her hands on his shoulders. His muscles were bunched tight beneath her fingers and she marveled at the strength emanating from him. She'd touched him before, while he'd worked with her on self-defense, and he had touched her. But not like this. Nothing like this.

The need rose from deep within her and she longed to run her hands over his arms, down his chest. His body was like a flame against her and she was drawn to it, dizzy with the masculine scent and feel of his skin. She sensed the struggle waging within Kane, felt the tension that was building steadily between them. When his hand moved slowly up her back, she caught her lower lip between her teeth, holding back the moan she felt deep in her throat.

A woman had never felt so soft in his arms before, so vulnerable. So damn sexy. Desire for her pounded in his blood and he wanted to crush her against him. It was the darkness, he decided. The night brought out foolish desires, released unfulfilled longings, let loose the fire that burned deep. A fire that could consume a man if he let it.

Her hair tumbled down her back and he caught the soft mass of curls in his hands, combing his fingers upward as he tightened his hold, gently and insistently pulling her head back. Even as he lowered his mouth to hers, he called himself a fool ten times over.

Her lips were moist and parted, eager for him. He cupped her head in his hands and pulled her closer, tasting her deeper, afraid he might never get enough. The moan from deep in Allison's throat sent him over the edge. He slid his hands down her back and over her hips, then lifted her with one hand while he parted her thighs with the other. She gasped as he pulled her to the edge of the seat and fitted her intimately with his body. Her arms wound around his neck and she met the thrust of his tongue with wild abandon, pressing her breasts against him and moving her body with the rhythm of their kiss.

He tugged at the belt of her robe and it fell open. He ran his hands up her long legs, pausing at the whisper-thin panties she wore, then moved up to her breasts. This time, as he filled his hands with her soft flesh, it was Kane who moaned. His thumbs circled her beaded nipples and she whimpered, pressing herself more fully into his hands.

God, how he wanted her. More than he'd ever remembered wanting a woman. But then, it was impossible to even remember another woman with Allison in his arms. It was impossible to even think.

And it was that thought that suddenly stopped him. She was a client, for God's sake, he was supposed to be protecting her, not taking her in the back seat of a car like some kind of sex-crazed teenager. Furious with himself, he took Allison by the arms and set her away from him.

"What—?"

The confusion—and need—he heard in her voice nearly had him reaching for her again. But he couldn't. He didn't dare touch her. Nothing, not his duty or his conscience would stop him if he touched her again. He moved away, then stepped out of the van. "You shouldn't have come down here," he said tightly.

She was silent for a moment, then he heard the soft rustle of her robe as she pulled it around her. She reached up and turned on the overhead light. Her eyes were narrowed with anger as she stared at him. "You are a son of a bitch."

She turned away from him then and reached under the seat where she'd dropped the doll. She stepped out of the van, her shoulders squared and chin lifted, and moved past him as if he weren't even there.

Fists clenched tight, he watched her go, praying like hell she'd keep that thought in mind.

Allison stood under the shade of a tall pine in the middle of the park, watching Kane struggle to corral ten rambunctious children into two straight lines for a water-balloon toss. He might as well have been trying to dig a hole in the ocean. For every two he'd position, three others would run off. When Courtney dropped her balloon and it splattered on the ground, Tommy Burns thought the game had begun and threw his, hitting Kane smack in the face as he bent to comfort a crying Courtney. Allison stifled a laugh as Kane slowly straightened, water dripping down his face and soaking the front of his blue long-sleeved shirt. With a desperate look in his eyes, he turned to Allison for assistance, but she simply smiled, waving as she leaned back against the tree.

Revenge is sweet, after all, she decided.

It wasn't as if she'd planned to put Kane in charge of picnic games, it had just sort of happened. The kids were all gathered round, Kane standing to the side unloading the cooler from the van, and she just couldn't resist. When she'd made the announcement that Kane would be leading the games, all the children had cheered excitedly. He was stuck and he knew it. The expression on his face said it all.

After what he'd done to her last night, leaving her hanging like he had, she hadn't the least bit of remorse. Even now, as she thought of his kiss, his hands on her skin, she felt the rise of a blush on her cheeks. Good Lord, what had come over her? She'd nearly begged the man to make love to her—right there in the darkness, in the back seat of a van, no less. She closed her eyes in humiliation. A man she hardly knew.

And yet, when he'd pulled her against him, it had felt so

right, as if she'd known him forever. She'd felt no hesitation, only a sense of belonging, that she was exactly where she should be. When he slipped his body between her legs and pressed his arousal tightly against her thighs, she felt an excitement she'd never experienced before and she'd gloried in the fact that he wanted her as badly as she wanted him.

Sighing, she leaned her head back against the tree trunk. If nothing else, at least she had that satisfaction. He *had* wanted her. No doubt about that.

How she'd managed to face him early this morning for her lessons she'd never know, but she had. Neither one of them mentioned the night before and she'd done her best to act as if nothing had happened. She'd blocked every move, practiced every kick; the same things they'd worked on, plus a couple of new moves. He was the teacher, she the student. Nothing more. But the strain of pretense was weighing on her. She had to face him again tomorrow, the day after that, and every day until this damn situation was over. The thought of his hands on her, pressing her against him was almost too much to bear.

"Allison, will you be my partner in the three-legged race?"

She opened her eyes at the insistent tug on her arm. It was Courtney, and the smile on the child's face was all that Allison needed to forget about her own problems for the moment.

"Of course I'll be your partner, sweetheart," she said, bending down to give the child a hug. "Come on, I'll race you over."

Kane watched as Allison and Courtney ran toward him. Client or no client, he decided, he was going to strangle Allison. The front of his shirt was still drenched from

Tommy's misguided balloon, one of the little girls was crying because she'd stepped in gum, and trying to get the rest of the kids to hold still to pair off for a three-legged race was like trying to pull a feather out of a tornado. As he bent down to tie two little girls' legs together, one of them shrieked loudly in his ear. He winced, certain he'd never hear from that ear again.

"Problem?"

Allison knelt down in front of him, smiling just a little too widely and a little too sweetly. He stood, shaking off the high-pitched ring in his ear. "Nothing a hearing aid won't correct."

She laughed. "And you probably thought watching over me was going to be an easy job, didn't you?"

"Easy?" He held out a hand and helped her up. "Jumping out of a plane is easy, scaling a twelve-foot wall with a thirty-pound knapsack is easy, even digging trenches in a 115° desert is easy. But watching over you—" he tried not to look at her lips, tried not to remember how only a few hours ago they'd been so eager against his own "—watching you is by far the most difficult thing I've ever had to do."

Lifting her chin, she met his gaze. Her eyes deepened to a seductive shade of smoky green. He fought back the tightening in his groin.

"Good," she said flatly, then turned and walked away.

Gritting his teeth, Kane moved to the next set of children and tied their legs. He *was* going to strangle the woman. Soon.

When he finished tying the next pair of kids together, Kane made a careful sweep of the park's perimeter. Tony stood on the outer edge of the picnic area, casually leaning against the trunk of an oak. Kane glanced his way and the man nodded that everything was all right. Nonetheless, Kane took in the surrounding people in the park: a young mother with a toddler on a blanket, an elderly couple reading at a park table, and what appeared to be a few college kids playing an impromptu game of football. When his gaze finally came around to one child sitting on a park bench away from all the others, Kane frowned.

It was Billy.

A strange ache filled Kane's chest as he stared at the boy. He knew what it felt like to not fit in, the pain of being different from everyone else. To wait for someone who was never going to return...

He walked over to Billy and sat beside him. "Hey, sport. Don't you want to be in the three-legged race?"

Billy shook his head and stared at the ground. "I'm not supposed to run around till my ear gets better."

Kane knew how and why Billy had needed ear surgery, but he refused to think about that now. Maybe later, in the gym, he'd vent his anger at the person who'd hurt this child, but not now. "Well, I need help tying legs and judging the winners, and then I could use a hand setting up the croquet game after lunch. Can you help me with all that?"

Billy looked up and nodded. Enthusiasm lighted the boy's dark brown eyes. "Yeah, I could do that."

"Great." He ruffled the child's short hair. "Let's do it."

The three-legged race was complete chaos, with more spills and tumbles than actual racing, but the kids had a great time. Allison avoided Kane as best she could, but when she and Courtney had fallen during the race, he was there, helping her up, and the simplest touch from him was enough to send her skin tingling and her pulse racing.

When the kids were all settled at the picnic table with their lunch and two more counselors from the center showed up, Allison grabbed a plate of sandwiches and made her way over to Tony. She intentionally avoided looking at Kane, but she felt the heat of his gaze burn into her back as she crossed the grassy field toward the other man.

"Thought you might like something to eat." She handed the plate to Tony.

Smiling, he accepted the food. "Thanks."

Tony was a handsome man, she acknowledged. No doubt his dark Italian looks and flashing smile had left a trail of broken hearts. And though she liked Tony, she was strangely immune to his charm.

Sighing, she leaned against the tree, determined not to look back at Kane. "Not exactly an exciting assignment," she said, "following me to work and sitting around in your car all day."

Tony laughed. "It beats sitting in a viewing room monitoring the lobby of the pavilion. At least I can see blue sky once in a while." He looked up at the sky and the clouds that had clustered overhead. "When it's not raining, anyway."

Because she couldn't help herself, Allison glanced over her shoulder. Kane was frowning sternly at her, his hand wrapped tightly around a cup of soda, oblivious to the fact that Tommy Burns was presently squeezing mustard into that cup. She couldn't wait to see Kane's face when he took a drink. Smiling, she turned back to Tony. "Tony, what do you think of Kane?"

He chewed thoughtfully. "Keeps to himself mostly, but seems like an okay guy. Has a way of looking at you that says more than words ever could."

Allison understood exactly what Tony meant. With the slightest shift of expression, Kane could either intimidate or seduce.

Tony took a swallow from the soda. "Lord help you if he thinks your mind isn't one hundred percent on your job. He's already replaced one of the men on the night watch at the house because the guy lit a match."

She stared at Tony incredulously. "He fired a man for lighting a match?"

"If someone were watching the house, it would have given away his position. The guy should have known better."

She couldn't believe it. Someone lost his job because of her. "But how could he—"

"Courtney's asking for you."

She turned at the sound of Kane's terse voice. He stood behind her, staring right through her at Tony, his gaze hard and narrowed. Tony straightened, gulping down the bite of sandwich in his mouth.

Allison would have loved to ignore Kane, but she was afraid if she did it might make problems for Tony. Gritting her teeth, she turned on her heels and stalked back to the kids, cursing Kane the entire way. How could a man be so gentle one moment, as she'd seen him be with Billy and the other kids, and such a jerk the next?

By the time she cleared away lunch, Allison's temper had reached a boiling point. Needing some physical activity to burn off her anger, she gathered a few of the kids and a kickball, then stormed as far away from Kane as she could get. Involved in the game, she managed to calm down and was actually enjoying herself when one of the boys kicked the ball back behind the brick building that contained the washrooms. Laughing, she ran around the building to retrieve the ball.

And ran smack into the barrel-sized chest of a man she'd never seen before.

Five

The faint smell of alcohol struck Allison as a pair of beefy arms closed around her. The sick feeling in her stomach intensified as she realized how huge the man was. Not tall, but stocky and muscular, with a neck as thick as a bulldog. She pushed against him, but she might as well have attempted to blow down a brick wall.

"Oh, mama," he said. "I've been waiting for you."

Don't panic. Don't panic. Don't panic, she repeated over and over what Kane had taught her. *Think.*

But she couldn't think. She was too terrified. *Dammit, Kane! Where are you?* She glanced over her shoulder, but no one could see her from here and she'd only been gone a second or two, hardly enough time for anyone to notice. She tried to yell, but the man held her so tightly she could barely breathe.

"What'cha got there?" Allison heard someone say and

watched as a second man sauntered up. He was young, wearing a torn T-shirt that said Seattle University. He carried the ball she'd run after, tossing it from hand to hand.

"I found her and she's all mine," her captor said, and his unshaved face scraped against Allison's cheek. "Think the dorm warden will let me keep her? It don't look like she eats much."

Dorm warden? Allison realized suddenly, with a small sense of relief, that these *men* were really no more than kids from the local university. But kids or not, this guy had her in a bear hug and she didn't like it one little bit.

Gritting her teeth, she calmed herself enough to assess the situation. The easiest way to break out would be to stomp on his instep and run like hell when he let her go. But he had her hoisted off the ground, with her arms pinned at her sides. She squirmed furiously, trying to get a foothold on the ground. And the more she squirmed, the tighter he held her.

"Let go of me," she managed to choke out, but her words were no more than a tight whisper and held little threat.

"But, baby, I love you." He chuckled. "You can't leave me. I'd die of a broken heart."

"Let her go."

Both men looked up at the sound of the quiet threat. They'd been too involved with Allison to see the other man walk up behind them. Kane's words had been spoken softly, but the strength and the power behind them had both men frozen.

Kane moved beside the man holding Allison. "Let her go," he repeated, "or a broken heart will be the least of your worries."

Eyes narrowed, his gaze hard and intense, Kane stared

at the man. When he finally released Allison, she stumbled back, rubbing at her arms.

The two men faced Kane. Allison could do little more than watch. Her legs were too shaky to go for Tony, and she still hadn't found her voice.

The kid with the ball drew in a deep breath to emphasize the size of his chest. The man who had been holding Allison seemed a little less sure, but he lifted his chin in a challenging gesture. They both took a step toward Kane.

Kane looked at both men, his stance seemingly casual. But Allison knew better. She could feel the energy radiating from Kane. It was dark and angry. Savage.

"You don't want to do this," was all he said, but once again, the absolute conviction in his voice had the other men faltering. Allison recognized the look that had entered the two men's eyes. Uncertainty. Fear.

The silence stretched, grew tight, then tighter still.

At last, the kid with the torn T-shirt relaxed his shoulders. "We didn't mean no harm," he said, tossing the ball to Allison.

The man who'd held Allison smiled hesitantly. "I was just messin' around. I wouldn't have hurt your girlfriend, mister."

They were backing away now, shrugging their shoulders. Mumbling an apology to Allison, they turned and sauntered back to a small group of their friends across the park.

Kane watched them go, then turned to Allison. She realized that the entire incident had lasted less than one minute. She started to smile at him, hoping to laugh the whole thing off, but his look cut her short.

"What the hell were you doing?"

She furrowed her brow. "What?"

"I said—" he moved toward her and the fury in his eyes

made her breath catch "—what the hell were you doing over here with these guys?"

"What was *I* doing?" She stared at him. "In case you hadn't noticed, I was being mauled."

"You left the picnic area and were out of eyesight."

"I was chasing a ball."

"Don't do it again," he said sharply. "You get me or Tony, but never let yourself out of our sight. Do you understand?"

He was angry, she realized incredulously. Angry at *her*. And he was talking to her as if she were a child. "I was only gone for a moment—"

"You were lucky this time, Allison. These were just a couple of kids messing around. Kids that I almost had to hurt." He took her roughly by the arm and pulled her close to him. "You see that tall bush over there? It would take less than four seconds to get you on the other side of it. I guarantee you that once you were there no one would ever see you again."

She glanced over at the thick shrubbery that could hide a person from the rest of the park. He was right, dammit. Someone could have easily gotten her over there. A sick feeling spread in the pit of her stomach.

Jerking her arm from his, she glared at him, determined not to let him know her knees were shaking. "You've made your point. I'll be more careful."

Her concession did little to appease him. He leaned over her, his eyes narrowed darkly. "And another thing, why the hell didn't you break that guy's kneecap or ruin his chances for a future family? We've gone over that hold, Allison. You should know it by now."

She couldn't believe it. He was actually reprimanding her. Clenching her hands into fists, Allison sucked in a deep, angry breath. It was bad enough she'd just been man-handled by some overanxious college kid, now she had to explain her lack of ability to Kane. She wanted to tell him the fault was his, because every time he tried to show her that move all she could think about was the feel of his body against her own and her concentration was shot to hell. But she'd been humiliated enough last night after he'd kissed her, and she had no intention of setting herself up for any-more. She turned to walk away, but he grabbed hold of her arm. Without thinking, she spun away from him—not only breaking his hold but shoving him back a step in the pro-cess.

Exactly as he'd taught her.

She saw the surprise register in Kane's eyes and knew he was seeing the same surprise in hers. A smile slowly tilted his lips.

Tony came running around the corner at that moment, the panic evident in the expression on his face. When he saw Kane and Allison, he stopped abruptly and the relief in his eyes was evident. "Everything all right?"

Kane glanced back at Allison. "Miss Westcott wandered into the arms of an overamorous admirer."

"I—I was in the bathroom," Tony started to explain. "I waved to you I was going in, I thought you acknowledged me and—"

"It's all right," Kane stopped Tony's apology. "No harm done. We're just going to have to tighten up a little bit."

Tighten up? Good God, Allison thought. She barely had a waking moment to herself as it was. If the man "tightened up" anymore she'd need a respirator. And based on the determined look in his eyes, there'd be no discussion on the subject right now.

Holding her tongue, she turned and picked up the ball, then walked away from both men. A woman walking a golden retriever passed by Allison, tugging the recalcitrant animal behind her. The dog pulled on its leash, obviously wanting to go in a different direction.

"I know how you feel, pooch," Allison muttered with a sigh and made her way back to the kids.

The report that Kane had compiled was at least three inches thick when Oliver Westcott returned from Los Angeles two days after the picnic. It contained the names and personal files of every person that Allison worked with, was friends with or had been friends with in the past three years. There was a listing of every function she'd been to, for the center and for her father, and the name of every man she'd been on a date with as far back as Kane could trace. Kane had read that part of the report with more interest than he would have liked to admit, but the files had shown nothing unusual and nothing to suggest their man was someone she knew personally.

Kane laid the report on Oliver's desk. It was already late in the day, nearly six o'clock, but Oliver had called Kane at the center and requested a meeting. Though he hated leaving Allison, he made arrangements for Tony to take her home and one of Westcott's men to follow.

"How was your trip to Los Angeles?" Kane asked, sitting in an armchair across from the other man.

An odd smile crossed Oliver's mouth, then disappeared. "Too damn hot," he muttered. "Imagine, only May and it hit ninety-five. I'll take rain and cool weather over that any day."

Kane waited while Oliver skimmed the first few pages of the report. After a few minutes, he closed the folder and frowned. "It doesn't look like we have much to go on here."

Kane shook his head. "I'm afraid not. It looks doubtful that our photographer is someone you or Allison know personally. I'm still gathering information on you, but the preliminary report shows no employees, ex-employees or associates with a grudge strong enough to come after you and no one with a previous criminal record beyond a misdemeanor."

Brow furrowed, Oliver sat back in his chair and loosened his tie. He looked tired. "What about the fingerprint on the film holder?"

"I'm still waiting on the report from Washington. I expect it in a day or two."

Oliver closed his eyes and sighed. "So we wait?"

"We wait."

After a long, quiet moment, Oliver looked at Kane. "You married, son?"

The question caught Kane off guard. "I was once."

"I always thought once was enough." Oliver swiveled his office chair to stare out the window. "Allison's mother was a special woman. After her death I buried myself in my work to ease my grief, and Allison lost herself in her dancing. She was quite good, you know."

Kane nodded. "I've read some of her reviews."

"I never even knew when she grew up, but one day I suddenly realized that my little girl was a beautiful woman."

"Yes, sir," Kane said uncomfortably. Of all the things he knew, he was painfully aware of Allison as a woman.

The phone buzzed and Oliver picked it up. "Yes, Shirley, go ahead and put her on." A pause, then "No, no bother at all."

Kane watched that curious smile appear on Oliver's mouth again. So it was a woman, Kane noted, holding back his own smile. Allison's father had met someone in Los Angeles. Not just met her, Kane realized as he listened, but had apparently brought her back to Seattle with him.

Acting as if he'd suddenly remembered something, Kane reached into the pocket of his sport coat and scribbled nonsense in the notepad he pulled out while Oliver talked quietly on the phone.

Trying not to listen, Kane forced his thoughts on his work. Allison would be home by now, probably in the shower. She always showered when she got home. An image of her flashed in his mind. Naked, with water splashing down on her back while she ran a soapy washcloth over her shoulders, down her breasts, over her stomach...

The notepad flipped out of his hands. Kane silently cursed his thoughts and the instant reaction his body was having. Dammit, anyway. It was getting more difficult by the day to keep his mind—and his hands—off her. He'd managed to keep his distance after the picnic, and she'd been so mad at him over his reprimand that she'd barely said more than a few terse words, though she had continued with their lessons.

But it was still there between them. The anticipation, the awareness, the sense that something was going to happen. He knew it, and he knew she knew it. How long they could ignore it he had no idea.

Oliver hung up the phone, clearing his throat and straightening his tie as he swiveled back around to face Kane. "Would you mind if we cut this short?" he asked, glancing at his watch. "I have another appointment in a few minutes."

Kane didn't ask her name. He'd have to, but not now. "Of course."

"Oh, and Kane—" Oliver seemed strangely awkward "—would you please tell Allison that I won't be home tonight, I, uh, have a lot of business to catch up on. Tell her I'll come by the center tomorrow before I leave for the Arizona seminar."

Kane stood and shook Oliver's hand. "I'll tell her."

He turned to leave, stopping at the door when Oliver called to him.

"You're doing a good job, son," the older man said. "Just make sure my little girl doesn't get hurt."

Just make sure my little girl doesn't get hurt.

Those words stuck in Kane's mind the entire way home. He drove faster than he should have and cursed profusely at a driver who cut him off. Even after he parked the car in the garage and checked everything with the men outside the house the words were still repeating themselves. Over and over. Like a damned broken record.

Irritable beyond reason, Kane swung open the door from the garage to the house and headed toward the kitchen, assuming he'd find Allison there preparing dinner. She wasn't. He started for the stairs, but when he heard the music he stopped and listened. Soft and low, classical, it was coming from the rec room.

He knew instinctively that he should walk away, run even, but an indefinable force drew him and he could have no more walked away than he could have stopped the sun from rising. He moved toward the music, his heart pounding in his chest, his blood pounding in his temples.

He opened the door and the room was filled with her, with her movement. She was dressed in a black leotard, as if she'd intended to match the mood of the music. Violins, mournful and slow, carried her and she followed the rhythm of the strings, her expression intent, focused on some invisible point. The mirrors reflected her and he stood, mesmerized, transfixed, surrounded by her image. Her arm lifted, stretched as softly and graceful as a curtain in the breeze. She raised on her toes, held her pose, then bent one leg smoothly before slowly stretching it behind her.

Though he'd been to the ballet, Kane could honestly admit he'd never really paid attention. Now, standing here watching Allison, he felt the vibrancy of the dance, the beauty. The passion. And though it was obvious the steps she was moving through were difficult, she mastered them with an elegance that would have made a butterfly envious. She spun slowly, arms arched at her sides, letting the violins carry her, then lifted her hands and face to the ceiling. Her hair was knotted at the nape of her head and the smooth, slender curve of her neck was the most erotic sight that Kane had ever seen in his life.

His throat was dry, his chest tight. *Quite good,* Oliver had said about his daughter's dancing. Good God, had the man ever watched her? She was more than "quite good." She was extraordinary. Stunning.

And she sure as hell was no little girl.

She spun again, moving into a jump. She cried out as she landed, falling on her knee. Closing her eyes in pain, Allison sat on the wooden floor and bent her head over her knee, drawing in a slow, unsteady breath.

He went to her, knelt down beside her. Allison's head came up sharply as she realized she wasn't alone.

"You are incredible," was all he could think to say.

She shook her head. "I can't even do a pirouette anymore without ending up in a pile on the floor."

His fingers moved over her cheek and along the smooth line of her jaw. Her skin was soft as warm silk. "No, Allison," he said quietly, "you're incredible just as you are."

He thought of her fierce determination, her compassion for others, the beauty inside her that was like a tall, cool glass of water to a parched, burning throat. All he had to do was drink....

Allison closed her eyes as Kane's mouth slowly lowered to hers. She was still reeling from the surprise of seeing him, and now, as he gently teased her lower lip, she couldn't even breathe. Pleasure streaked through her. Exquisite, sweet pleasure. She moved toward him, deepening the kiss, matching the stroke of his tongue with her own. His arms came around her, forcefully but not rough. She slid her hands up his arms, then over his shoulders, ignoring the urgent whisper from the back of her mind telling her to stop.

His hands moved over her body like a liquid flame, melting away the last of her resolve. It didn't matter to her that this was foolish. It was just as foolish to deny what she was feeling. And whether Kane would admit it or not, he was feeling it, too. There was more between them than simple lust. She knew it. She had learned long ago to trust her feelings, to go with her instincts, and as surely as she gave herself up to her music and let it take her, she now gave herself up to Kane.

He was powerless to stop what was happening. God help him, he didn't want to stop. He'd never ached like this before, never lost touch with reality. But Allison *was* reality and she was in his arms, her soft body pressed against him, her lips warm and passionate under his.

He gathered her against him and with his arms wrapped tightly around her he lowered them both to the floor, pulling her on top of him. She ran her hands over him and a low, guttural moan rose from deep in his throat. He felt his blood rushing through his body, faster and hotter than he'd ever known before, and the exquisite pain of wanting this woman blocked out all other thoughts. He was trapped, caught in a web of desire, and if he struggled he'd only entangle himself tighter. Give in to it, he told himself, give in.

Allison trembled when Kane's lips moved, first to her neck, then downward. She caught her lower lip between her teeth as his mouth found her breast and teased the hardened nipple through the fabric of her leotard. She squirmed against him, moaning softly, wanting him to take her into his mouth, to feel his tongue and his hands on her.

And of all the things she didn't want to be, it was interrupted.

"Kane," she gasped weakly.

His fingers slid over the curve of her hip. "Hmm?"

"What—" she drew in a sharp breath when his hand moved over her buttocks "—what time is my father coming home?"

He knew she was saying something to him, something he didn't want to hear, something that he knew would pull him from this fantasy he was having. But she repeated her question and the words sank her. Her father. Oliver.

Just make sure my little girl doesn't get hurt.

He went still, swearing vehemently at himself before he slowly rose, bringing both he and Allison to a sitting position. He held her shoulders tightly, struggling between pulling her back to him and pushing her away. "He's not coming home."

Allison smiled slowly. Her eyes were bright with passion, her lips still moist from his kiss. His resolve slipped, then he gritted his teeth and dropped his hands from her. "I shouldn't have done that. I'm sorry."

Her smile faded as she stared at him for a long moment. Her confused expression slowly turned to anger. "Not half as sorry as I am," she said and started to rise. He grabbed her by the shoulders, holding her back.

"Allison, listen to me. I'm not used to explaining myself, but I'm going to try."

She lifted one eyebrow. "Oh, thank you so much. I'm so honored."

Kane didn't blame her for being angry. She had every right. But she couldn't possibly be as angry at him as he was at himself. He drew in a deep breath, then slowly released it. "Right now, I want you more than I've ever wanted another woman in my life."

Her laugh was sarcastic. "Considering you just pushed me away—for the second time—that's really not saying much."

"Dammit, Allison." He tightened his hold on her. "It has nothing to do with you." He shook his head. "No, that's not right, it has everything to do with you. I can't think clearly around you. You make me forget what I'm supposed to be doing, why I'm here."

She stared at him, waiting for him to talk.

He let go of her then and stood, raking his hands through his hair as he moved to the cassette player and turned off the music. The silence echoed in the room.

He turned and faced her. "You distract me, Allison. Distraction leads to mistakes and I can't afford to make mistakes."

"What mistakes have you made?"

His jaw tightened. "That first day we were driving to the center I did miss my turn. I was thinking about you."

Her brow lifted, but she said nothing.

"And then at the picnic I let that kid get his grimy paws on you."

"But that wasn't—"

"Yes, it *is* my fault," he said sharply. "I'm responsible for you. I'm here to make sure nothing happens to you. I can't do that when I'm not focused."

Her lips thinned. "And I suppose kissing me is a mistake, too?"

"The biggest one of all." He watched the anger flare in her eyes again, then added a little more softly, "Because now that I know what you taste like, what you feel like, it's going to be torture to keep away." He met her gaze and held it. "But I can't touch you again, Allison. I won't. Because I'm only human and if I do, there'll be no stopping."

"And what if I don't want you to stop?"

Her quiet declaration almost had him reaching for her again. Her honesty was one of the things that attracted him to her. Lord knew, he'd seen little of it in his life.

But he couldn't touch her, he didn't dare. Instead, he tightened his hands into fists and faced her. "I won't be here long, Allison," he said quietly. "Maybe only a few days. It's better this way for both of us."

Allison watched as he walked away from her and out of the room. She stared after him for a long time, trying to absorb his words. But she kept coming back to what she felt and what she knew in her heart.

You're a damn stubborn man, Thomas Kane, she whispered, then smiled slowly.

Whether he knew it or not, this was war.

Six

They were late.

Kane stood at the base of the stairs and for at least the third time in less than five minutes he stared at his watch. 7:16.

Frowning, he glanced at the top of the stairs. She'd told him to be ready at seven, and even from the short time that he'd known Allison, Kane had determined that she was probably the most punctual woman he'd ever met. Her lessons, work, appointments. It wasn't her nature to be late for anything. So what in the world was keeping her?

Hands in his pockets, he resumed his pacing. He told himself that the tension he felt had nothing to do with spending the evening with Allison at the fund-raising ballet and dinner for St. Martin's Center. It certainly wasn't as if they were going out on a date. For Kane, it was just part of his job.

He simply wanted to get there early. Before the crowd got too large. Kane hated the idea of being in a crowd with Allison. It would not only be difficult to keep a close eye on her, there were also too many variables in an uncontrolled environment.

And when it came to Allison, he thought with a sigh, there were enough variables as it was.

She'd been different somehow the past three days. He couldn't quite put his finger on it, but she'd seemed more…distant…yet, at the same time, more cordial. As if she were entertaining a houseguest or business client. When they spoke it was superficial chitchat. She barely gave him a second glance while she was working and even during her morning lessons her concentration had improved. Which was more than he could say for his own.

Of course, that was what he wanted. To keep their relationship professional. He'd told her he couldn't become involved, and obviously she'd listened. It was best for both of them. He certainly shouldn't be annoyed by her indifference. If anything, he should be relieved.

So why, then, for the past three days, did he feel the need to spend an extra thirty minutes on the weight bench and fifteen more with the punching bag?

He glanced at his watch again. It couldn't take her this long to get ready. She was beautiful as it was. What could she possibly do to improve on her appearance? Maybe she'd simply lost track of the time and needed a reminder. He started up the stairs, but hadn't taken more than three steps before a knock at the front door stopped him. Muttering an oath, he turned to answer it.

A young man dressed in a chauffeur's uniform stood on the porch.

"Good evening, sir." The chauffeur slid his hat off, revealing wavy blond hair. "Your limousine is here."

Kane frowned at the man. He hadn't liked the idea of taking a limousine. But the center's major benefactor, Michael Peterson, had ordered them for the entire staff at St. Martin's.

"You were supposed to be here fifteen minutes ago, Kolowski," Kane snapped, taking his irritation out on the man.

Obviously surprised that Kane knew his name, the driver shifted uncomfortably. Kane not only knew the man's name, he knew his mother and brother's names. There was no way that Kane would have allowed Allison to get in a limousine without checking out the driver first.

"I'm sorry, sir." Kolowski fingered his hat nervously. "I was stuck in—"

Eyes wide, jaw slack, Kolowski froze as he stared at something behind Kane's back. Frowning, Kane turned, then went absolutely still as he watched Allison glide down the stairs.

Stunning.

It was the first and only thought he was capable of. She was absolutely stunning. Her dress fit her like a glove of black lace. The sleeves were long and sheer and the heart-shaped neckline dipped dangerously low, hugging the fullness of her breasts. Her hair was swept up off her slender neck; pearl-and-diamond teardrops glittered from her earlobes. A high slit up the side of her dress revealed her incredible long legs. He felt as if he'd been punched in the gut without warning.

"Good evening, gentlemen. Sorry to keep you waiting."

He barely heard what she said. All he could hear was the quiet swish of silk against lace and the soft click of her black high heels as she moved across the marble entry. It was impossible to take his eyes off her.

She smiled sweetly at Kane, then raised her hand to tuck back a loose curl. The movement lifted her breasts and the soft, tempting swell nearly had him groaning out loud. Kane's throat was too dry to speak, but it didn't matter. He'd forgotten how.

Allison turned to the driver and held out her hand. "I'm Allison Westcott."

The driver stared at her hand for a long moment, then hesitantly shook it. "Brian," he squeaked out. "Brian Kolowski."

When Brian didn't let go of Allison's hand, Kane's jaw tightened. Grinning, the driver glanced over at Kane. His smile quickly faded as he caught the murderous look in Kane's eyes. He released Allison's hand and cleared his throat.

"I'll wait with the car," he mumbled quickly and made his getaway.

Kane struggled to gather his composure as Allison turned and retrieved a small black sequined purse from the entry table.

"Ready?" she asked, facing him.

The first time Kane had jumped out of an airplane, the instructor had asked him the same thing. He'd never forget the sharp, sick clenching of his stomach and the fear of wondering how far he'd have to fall before he hit the ground. He had exactly the same feeling now.

"Ready," he answered tightly and offered his arm.

Allison laid her hand on Kane's arm and hoped like hell that he wouldn't notice her fingers were trembling. Walking calmly down that stairway had been ten times more difficult than any opening-night performance. Based on the approval in Kane's expression as he stared at her, however, it was certainly worth it.

But there was something more. Something in his eyes she hadn't seen before. A hungry, possessive look that almost frightened her, a look that made her heart skip wildly and had her wondering if it was indeed wise to wake a sleeping beast.

For three days she'd pretended nonchalance. In the morning, when he worked with her on self-defense, she forced herself to concentrate completely on the lesson instead of the feel of his hands on her skin or the hard length of his body pressed against hers. At the center she focused on her work and the children, and in the evening she kept to herself.

It was the night that betrayed her.

At night, her thoughts were wild and wanton, refusing to be caged in denial. At night, she would wake with the sensation of his lips on hers, with the touch of his hands on her breasts. She could see him clearly, his body poised and ready, his eyes dark and intense as he lowered himself over her....

Shaking off the thought, she stole a glance at him now as he helped her into the limo. He was devastating in a tuxedo. With his dark hair, deep blue eyes and that rugged masculinity of his, there wouldn't be a woman in the crowd who wouldn't want to be in her place tonight.

She sighed silently, dipping her head as she stepped into the back seat. As if her situation were anything to be envied. She'd been uprooted from her apartment, had twenty-four-hour guards, and couldn't even step outside without worrying that some "crazy" might suddenly grab her. Every woman's typical, run-of-the-mill fantasy, she thought sarcastically.

Leaning back in her seat, Allison watched Kane through the back window as he stood outside and gave directions to Tony, who looked quite handsome himself in a tuxedo. She wished it was Tony she was attracted to instead of Kane. Lord knew, her life would be easier, and based on the occasional look that Tony gave her, a lot less disappointing. Kane was wrong for her; she knew it. He wasn't a man to stay in one place. He'd been honest with her about that. He'd never once given her hope or led her on.

Yet there was something between them. Something physical, of course, but something even more than simple lust. It shimmered under the surface, waiting, and whatever it was, no amount of logic or reason could argue it away. Lord knew, she'd certainly tried.

Kane slid into the back seat beside her and signaled the driver to leave. He was quiet while they pulled away from the house and headed for the highway. He stared out the window, his jaw tight and eyes narrowed, and if Allison could have touched the tension in the car she was sure that sparks would have flown.

"Something wrong?" she asked.

Nothing a long, cold shower wouldn't take care of, Kane thought. He turned and let his gaze slide down the length of her, the slender curve of her neck, the rise of her breasts, the long, long legs in black silk stockings. Just looking at her aroused him to the point of pain. Frowning, he turned back to the window, deciding that a shower in a blizzard wouldn't be cold enough. "You're not to leave my side tonight."

"I'm afraid that's not possible. Michael made arrangements for me to sit with him months ago."

"I unmade them," Kane said, reaching for a glass from the limo bar. "You'll be sitting with me."

"You did what?" She straightened in her seat. "This is going too far, Kane. I have a life, you know, and you have no right—"

"Yes, I do." He cut her off. "I can't watch you from the back of a dark, crowded room. Whether you like it or not, you're with me for the evening."

"Maybe you ought to just handcuff me," Allison said sarcastically.

He smiled at her. "It could be arranged."

Fuming, Allison folded her arms and turned away to stare out the window. She watched the light dance off the water as they crossed over the sound. This fund-raiser was for the center, for her kids, and no one was going to ruin her evening, she resolved. Not even Kane.

Kane filled his glass with ice, then poured himself two fingers of whiskey from a crystal decanter. He wasn't going to drink it, he never drank on a job. He was just going to hold it, sniff it and look forward to getting himself good and plastered as soon as possible.

He settled back in his seat and couldn't stop himself from staring at the glimpse of leg revealed by the open slit of Allison's dress. For one crazy moment he imagined telling the driver to ignore his exit and just keep driving—he didn't care where. Anywhere that he could be alone with Allison, where he could strip that dress off her and pull her beneath him and ease the ache that was burning a hole in his gut. The hell with his job and his damn responsibility. He'd have her and maybe then he could get her out of his system and out of his mind. His hand tightened on the glass and he did battle with himself not to down the contents in one gulp.

It was going to be a long night. He tore his gaze from Allison. A very long night.

* * *

Strains of Tchaikovsky slowly filled the darkened auditorium. The room fell silent and every head turned to the stage, watching as the dancers glided gracefully onto the set. Every head except one.

Kane scanned the auditorium, searching the darkness for anything or anyone that might look suspicious. He had a man at both exits, one more in the lobby, and Tony was outside in the parking lot. When it came to Allison, Kane was taking no chances.

He sat back in his seat, watching her from the corner of his eye. She'd leaned forward, intent on the performance, a slight smile on her lips as she followed the dancers' movements. He could see the excitement in her eyes, the delight, and he found himself smiling with her.

It should have been Allison up there, he thought. He knew she could move every bit—no *more*—beautifully and gracefully than any dancer on that stage. She had the innate ability, the determination. The passion.

And now, as he watched her, he understood for the first time exactly what Allison had lost when she hurt her knee. She'd lost a part of herself, of her very soul. And the only thing that could come close to replacing that loss for her was her work at the center.

Ninety minutes later, after the applause died down and the prima ballerina left the stage, Allison turned to Kane. "Tell me that wasn't wonderful," she said breathlessly.

He grinned at her. "It was wonderful."

Light danced in her green eyes as she took hold of his arm and hugged it. They sat there, smiling at each other, and it felt to Kane as if they were the only two people in the world, sharing something important and special. He covered her hand with his and as they stared at each other, their smiles slowly faded.

He wanted to say something. Something important. He just wasn't sure what it was. "Allison," he said softly, leaning toward her—

"Allison!"

The single swear word that Kane uttered was earthy but reflected Allison's feeling regarding the intrusion, as well. Kane pulled his hand away from her and she turned impatiently. It was Michael. He waved as he caught her eye and pushed through the crowd toward her.

Sighing inwardly, she stood and made her way to the aisle. Kane followed closely, his hand on her elbow. When Michael bent and kissed her cheek, she could have sworn she felt Kane stiffen.

"Allison, I'm so glad I found you. I was worried when I got your note you wouldn't be able to join me."

Allison shot a look at Kane, but his expression never changed. "I'm sorry, Michael. I didn't have time to call. My, uh, cousin—" she touched Kane's arm "—came into town unexpectedly."

Kane raised an eyebrow at Allison's explanation. She smiled at him. "Thomas Kane, this is Michael Peterson."

Michael shook Kane's hand, but kept his attention on Allison. "You look absolutely incredible in that dress."

"Why, thank you. It's so nice of you to say so." She cast a glance at Kane. At least *someone* was willing to tell her.

When Michael's gaze lingered on Allison's neckline, Kane's hands clenched into fists. He started to take a step forward, then remembered where he was and why he was here.

What the hell's the matter with me? He'd been with lots of beautiful women, and never once had he objected if another man showed his admiration. And he couldn't exactly bite the head off every man who talked to or looked at Allison tonight. It would look like a war zone if he did.

She was making him lose control. And that was something he could never allow. Her life, and his sanity, depended on it.

"I insist you both join me for a drink." Michael took Allison by the arm and led her up the aisle.

Kane stared at Michael's back, knowing that if he stepped on the man's foot just right, he could disable him for the rest of the night. Allison, however, might take exception and, of course, it wouldn't be very professional.

He stopped suddenly. For some reason he couldn't explain or define, the hair on the back of his neck rose.

Scanning the crowd, Kane took in every face, looking for anything unusual, anything to explain the feeling that someone was watching them. He saw nothing out of the ordinary, just the bustle of people as they moved, laughing and talking, toward the lobby. Gradually the sensation disappeared.

Wary, Kane stayed close to Allison, and when they reached the reception room he smoothly maneuvered himself between her and Michael.

"Allison tells me you're a mutual-fund manager," Kane said, ignoring Allison's glare. They both knew she hadn't told him a thing about Michael.

Michael smiled. "That's right."

"Biotech, right?"

"Why, yes," Michael answered with surprise. "I hadn't realized Allison was so well informed."

Allison shifted uncomfortably under Michael's perusal. She had no idea what Kane was up to, but she was going to murder him. Violently. For the moment, though, she thought it best to smile sweetly. "I've always found mutual funds fascinating, Michael. I thought you knew that."

"She's a storehouse of information," Kane went on. "In fact, just today she was telling me that the FDA disapproved that new drug, what's it called?" He rubbed his chin thoughtfully. "Oh, yes. Prilasac. But then, I'm sure you already knew that."

Michael's mouth dropped open. "Oh, uh, of course." He glanced frantically around the room. "Hey, how about I go get us some drinks? Won't take me a minute."

He was gone before they even answered. Allison stared after him, watching him walk right past the bar toward the telephones. She turned to Kane and frowned. "What was that all about?"

Kane shrugged. "Just passing on a little information, cousin."

Her frown deepened. "I thought that sort of thing was illegal."

"Of course not. It's common knowledge."

Allison knew there was nothing about Kane, or his knowledge, that was common. "I had the feeling you were trying to get rid of him."

Kane lifted his brow innocently. "Did you?"

"Yes," she answered with more annoyance than she'd intended to show. "I just don't understand why. You don't even know the man. What possible reason could you have to send him off on some wild-goose chase?"

"It wasn't a wild-goose chase." A waiter passed by, offering wine, and Kane snatched a glass for Allison. As he handed her the wine, his gaze held steady with hers. "And besides, I didn't like the way he looked at you."

Allison's heart began to pound, a heavy, deep thud that blocked out all other sound. Kane's fingers grazed hers as she accepted the glass, and she felt a jolt of electricity skitter up her arm. He couldn't be jealous. Not Kane. "Michael's just a friend. We don't, I mean, we aren't—"

"Lovers?"

Allison felt her cheeks flush at Kane's uncouth question. "Michael is one of the most charming and handsome men I know."

"And still you haven't—"

"No." She pressed her lips tightly together.

He leaned closer. "Why not?"

The tension between them increased to the point of being unbearable. The smell of Kane's after-shave, mixed with his own masculine scent, had her hand tightening on her glass. "In case you haven't noticed, I spend most of my time at the center. For now, that's all I need."

"Is it?"

She knew she should walk away, end this conversation right here. It wasn't going to lead to anything but frustration. But the deep tone of his voice closed around her like a velvet trap, pulling her steadily closer. He made her feel soft inside, light-headed, and she hated herself for her own weakness. And she suddenly hated him, too. "What do you want from me, Kane?"

Allison's question caught Kane off guard. He hadn't meant to let this conversation go so far. He hadn't meant to let *anything* with Allison go so far. And if the road to hell was paved with intentions, good or bad, he was well on his way. He took a step back, reminding himself he was here to do a job. But he knew he was only kidding himself. Because he *did* want something from Allison. And whatever it was, it scared the hell out of him.

She stared at him, and the look in her eyes made him feel as if a steel band were tightening around his chest.

"That's what I thought," she said quietly.

"Allison—"

She shook her head. "Let's forget it. I came here to have a good time."

She turned sharply, intending to join a group of her friends from the center, and nearly ran into a woman standing behind her.

"Caroline!"

Kane watched as Allison hugged a tall blonde dressed in a slinky black dress with gold sequins. Both women talked at once, and though he knew the woman was familiar he couldn't quite place her. After several minutes, Allison turned back to Kane.

"Caroline Petrova, this is Thomas Kane."

Caroline Petrova. He'd heard the name before. He felt suddenly foolish as he realized she was the prima ballerina that he'd watched for an hour and a half. Well, that he'd almost watched, if he hadn't been so absorbed in Allison.

Allison tossed back a swallow of wine, detesting the pang of jealousy that streaked through her as Kane fell into an easy conversation with Caroline. She'd never seen him so charming before. And he'd certainly never smiled at *her* like that.

Avoiding him hadn't gotten his attention, neither had throwing herself at him. He'd admitted that she distracted him when he was working, but the bottom line was that she was a responsibility to him. A job. Nothing more. Why was she wasting her time and energy?

She suddenly felt very tired. Tired of living under a microscope, tired of worrying about who was around the next corner, and tired of being a fool over a man who was so damn determined not to feel anything for her.

If only for a few minutes, she needed to get out of here. And she needed to be alone.

Excusing herself to Caroline, Allison handed her glass to a passing waiter and started to walk away. She'd nearly made it across the lobby when Kane stopped her.

"I thought I told you to stay by me," he said irritably.

She glanced down at Kane's hand on her arm, angry at herself for the response she felt from a simple touch. Lifting one brow, she smiled sweetly at him. "That's fine by me, but the other ladies might take exception."

When she nodded toward the hallway where the rest rooms were, Kane hesitated. Clearly, he didn't even like her going to the rest room without him.

"I'll be back in five minutes," she reassured him. "Maybe ten if the gossip's any good."

When he still hesitated, she sighed. "Kane, for God's sake, there are at least four hundred people here. I promise I'll scream if anyone touches me."

Frowning, Kane nodded and let go of her arm. She felt his gaze burn into her as she walked away. Once she turned down the hallway and was out of sight she waited a moment, then sneaked back and peeked around the corner. He was making his way across the lobby toward one of her father's security men. The man had a radio he was talking into.

It was the only chance she was going to get. Five minutes. That's all she wanted. She'd sit quietly in the limo, by herself, then sneak back in and no one would be the wiser. She made her way around the corner and bolted for the front entrance, hiding next to a tall man as he walked out.

Once she was outside, Allison felt as if a hundred pounds had been lifted from her shoulders. It was raining again and she took in a deep breath of damp night air, then walked quickly to the limo and slipped into the back seat.

The driver was sitting behind the wheel, listening to a baseball game on the radio. Though she was disappointed she wasn't alone, she had to take what she could get.

"I just needed a little break from the hubbub," she told him, closing the door behind her. "Just pretend I'm not here."

He started the engine, and surprised, Allison looked up at him. "No, I'm not ready to leave, yet, Brian—"

It wasn't Brian, she realized. Though he hadn't turned around, Allison could see that this man's hair was dark; his shoulders were wider, his neck thicker. She suddenly felt like an idiot. She must have gotten into the wrong limo.

"I'm sorry," she said, reaching for the door. "I must have the wrong—"

The car was already backing out as the man swung his arm around. Allison's eyes widened in terror as she realized he had a gun in his hand.

"You just sit back and enjoy the ride," he said hoarsely, accelerating in reverse. "Just do what I say and you won't get hurt."

An Important Message from the Editors

Dear Reader,

Because you've chosen to read one of our fine novels, we'd like to say "thank you"! And, as a special way to thank you, we're offering you a choice of two more of the books you love so well, and a surprise gift to send you – absolutely FREE!

Please enjoy them with our compliments...

Pam Powers

Peel off Seal and Place Inside...

EDITOR'S
FREE GIFT
SEAL
THANK YOU

What's Your Reading Pleasure...
ROMANCE? _OR_ SUSPENSE?

Do you prefer spine-tingling page turners OR heart-stirring stories about love and relationships? Tell us which books you enjoy – and you'll get 2 FREE "ROMANCE" BOOKS or 2 FREE "SUSPENSE" BOOKS with no obligation to purchase anything.

Choose "ROMANCE" and get **2 FREE BOOKS** that will fuel your imagination with intensely moving stories about life, love and relationships.

FREE!

Choose "SUSPENSE" and you'll get **2 FREE BOOKS** that will thrill you with a spine-tingling blend of suspense and mystery.

FREE!

Whichever category you select, your 2 free books have a combined cover price of $11.98 or more in the U.S. and $13.98 or more in Canada.

And remember. . . just for accepting the Editor's Free Gift Offer, we'll send you 2 books and a gift, ABSOLUTELY FREE!

YOURS FREE! We'll send you a fabulous surprise gift absolutely FREE, just for trying "Romance" or "Suspense"!

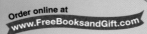

Order online at
www.FreeBooksandGift.com

THE EDITOR'S "THANK YOU" FREE GIFTS INCLUDE:

▶ 2 Romance OR 2 Suspense books

▶ An exciting surprise gift

YES! I have placed my Editor's "thank you" Free Gifts seal in the space provided at right. Please send me the 2 FREE books which I have selected, and my FREE Mystery Gift. I understand that I am under no obligation to purchase anything further, as explained on the back of this card.

PLACE
FREE GIFTS
SEAL
HERE

Check one:

| ROMANCE |
| 193 MDL EE3L 393 MDL EE3X |

| SUSPENSE |
| 192 MDL EE3W 392 MDL EE4A |

FIRST NAME

LAST NAME

ADDRESS

APT.#

CITY

STATE/PROV.

ZIP/POSTAL CODE

▶ DETACH AND MAIL CARD TODAY! ▶

© 1998 MIRA BOOKS

(ED1-SS-06)

The Reader Service — Here's How It Works:

Accepting your 2 free books and gift places you under no obligation to buy anything. You may keep the books and gift and return the shipping statement marked "cancel." If you do not cancel, about a month later we'll send you 3 additional books and bill you just $5.24 each in the U.S., or $5.74 each in Canada, plus 25¢ shipping & handling per book and applicable taxes if any.* That's the complete price and — compared to cover prices starting from $5.99 each in the U.S. and $6.99 each in Canada — it's quite a bargain! You may cancel at any time, but if you choose to continue, every month we'll send you 3 more books, which you may either purchase at the discount price or return to us and cancel your subscription.

*Terms and prices subject to change without notice. Sales tax applicable in N.Y. Canadian residents will be charged applicable provincial taxes and GST.

If offer card is missing write to: The Reader Service, 3010 Walden Ave., P.O. Box 1867, Buffalo, NY 14240-1867

BUSINESS REPLY MAIL
FIRST-CLASS MAIL   PERMIT NO. 717-003   BUFFALO, NY

POSTAGE WILL BE PAID BY ADDRESSEE

THE READER SERVICE
3010 WALDEN AVE
PO BOX 1341
BUFFALO NY 14240-8571

NO POSTAGE
NECESSARY
IF MAILED
IN THE
UNITED STATES

Seven

Kane tore out the front doors and raced down the steps as the limo was backing out of the parking space. Though he couldn't make out the driver's face through the darkened windows, Kane knew that it was not Brian Kolowski. The limo's back tires spun on the wet pavement, then squealed as the man floored the accelerator and sped off.

Kane screamed Allison's name as he raised his gun. He had maybe two seconds before the car would be out of range. Two seconds before Allison would be gone.

He aimed his gun and fired at the back left tire. He missed. Tightening his grip on his gun, he fired again. The tire popped and the car skidded, then crashed into another car that suddenly pulled in front of it. Tony's car, Kane realized. Though obviously dazed, Tony gave Kane the okay sign and waved him to go on. With his gun still in his hand, Kane ran to the limo and tore open the driver's door.

The driver's seat was empty, the passenger door open. Brian Kolowski was tied up on the front-seat floor. "You okay?" he shouted at Allison, who was sitting forward on the back seat, her hand on her temple.

"Yes." She nodded haltingly. "He went that way—" she pointed to the crowded parking lot "—between those cars."

Swearing profusely, Kane searched the darkened parking lot. He saw nothing, but he heard the squeal of tires and as he looked in the direction of the sound, he saw the taillights of a white import disappear around the corner.

Dammit! With Tony's car blocking the limo, there'd be no way he could catch the guy now.

But all that really mattered at this moment, Kane thought as he ran back to the limo, was that Allison was all right.

Still breathing heavily, Kane holstered his gun and opened the back door. Allison was leaning back in the seat, her eyes closed. Ignoring the crowd that was forming behind him, Kane slid in beside her and gathered her trembling body close to him.

"Are you all right?" he asked through ragged breaths.

Dazed, Allison laid her forehead against his chest and clutched the front of his jacket. "Oh sure, just another night out at the ballet," she said shakily.

Kane smiled with relief. At least she still had enough spunk to be sarcastic. Desperately he wanted to kiss her, to feel her mouth under his and know she was all right, but the most he could allow himself was to pull her closer to him and press his lips lightly to the top of her head.

"Did you get a good look at him?" he asked gently.

She shook her head. "He never really turned around. I just saw his eyes in the rearview mirror. They were terrifying. Dark. Piercing. Ominous.'' She shivered and tried to get closer to Kane, but he already had her flush against him.

She felt so small in his arms, so vulnerable. The bastard had almost gotten her, Kane thought. He'd almost succeeded. A murderous rage came over him and he had to close his eyes and draw in a slow, deep breath to ward it off. Now was not the time. Later, when he could work it off he'd vent his anger.

And speaking of anger... He took Allison by the shoulders and held her away from him. Her face was pale under the overhead light of the limo. ''What the hell were you doing out here?''

''I just needed a few minutes by myself,'' she said defensively.

The quiver in her chin almost had him pulling her to him again. Frustrated, he tightened his hold on her arms. ''Dammit, Allison, don't ever do that again. If Tony hadn't seen you come out and called it in to lobby security, you'd be long gone by now. Do you understand that?''

She went still in his arms. ''I don't think anyone understands that better than I do,'' she said quietly, then twisted out of his hold and rubbed her arms.

He felt like a heel, reprimanding her after what she'd been through. But dammit, he'd almost lost her and the thought of anyone laying one hand on her evoked emotions in him he could not allow to surface. Emotions that were much too dangerous to recognize.

A moan from the front seat reminded Kane that poor Brian was still on the floor. Shoulders squared, Allison turned away from him and stared out the window. He started to reach for her again, but pulled back when Brian moaned again. It was for the best, he knew. Because if he touched her again, he might not ever let go.

* * *

Two hours later, Allison stood in stocking feet at the base of the stairs and let out a slow sigh of exhaustion. It was nearly midnight, and to say it had been a hell of a night was the understatement of the century. The police had questioned both her and the limo driver, but neither one of them had been able to give a detailed description. All that Brian could remember was someone standing beside the limo rapping on the window and when he'd rolled it down a fist smashed into his face and everything went black. Not even Tony had seen the switch. And all that Allison could remember was her horrible consuming fear of the man holding the gun on her.

She shivered at the thought and sat on the bottom step of the stairs, dropping her shoes and rubbing her arms to ward off the sudden chill. The last hour—at Kane's insistence—had been spent at the hospital while a doctor examined her and Tony. They'd both been given a clean bill, though Allison's nerves were understandably shaky and Tony's left arm was bruised from the crash.

Rubbing her temple to clear away the ache in her head, Allison glanced toward the open front door where Kane was quietly speaking to one of his men on the porch. She stared at his silhouette in the darkness, feeling relief that he was here with her. She refused to allow herself to even think about what would have happened if he and Tony hadn't been there tonight. She closed her eyes, trying to blot out the image of that man staring at her in the rearview mirror....

"You okay?"

She jumped at the sound of Kane's voice, then sucked in a deep breath and nodded. "I was just going to bed now."

They stood and stared at each other for a long moment, neither one of them moving.

"Do you need anything?" he said finally. "The doctor prescribed some pills, or how about a drink?"

She shook her head. "I'm fine, Kane." She noted the deep furrow on his brow and the grim frown on his face. "Really."

The silence stretched taut between them, and for one brief instant she almost thought he might reach out to her. When he didn't, she swallowed her disappointment and stood.

"Good night," she said quietly, then slowly started up the stairs. A good night's sleep, that's all she needed. Everything would be fine in the morning. She had the day off. Maybe she'd dance a little, that always calmed her down, or maybe she'd go for a swim or—

Without warning, her legs crumbled beneath her. She heard the sound of crying, and realized with embarrassment that she was its source. She tried to stand up, to stop herself, but it was futile. *Damn.* Even as more tears came, she cursed herself. If only she could have made it to her room, if she could have broken down without Kane watching.

And then he was holding her, whispering something soft and sweet in her ear, pressing his lips to her cheek, then her forehead. He caressed her with his words and his mouth, then pulled her onto his lap and wrapped his arms around her.

"I'm so sorry," she managed between sobs, burying her face against his white shirt. "I could have gotten you or Tony killed tonight."

"But you didn't," he said softly. "All that matters is that you're all right."

"It was stupid, I know it. I just needed a minute alone."

He smoothed her hair back from her face. "Why didn't you tell me?"

"And what would you have done?" When he didn't answer, she looked up at him. "You see what I mean?"

He sighed. "I'm sorry, Allison. Until we catch this guy, and we will, I can't let you out of my sight." He smiled then and wiped a tear from her cheek with his thumb. "I've always wondered what the inside of a ladies' room looked like."

She laughed softly and laid her head on his shoulder. This was a side of Kane she'd never seen. Though he'd been gentle in the limo earlier, she'd felt the intensity in him, the energy coiled inside him. He was calmer now and his soft words and gentle touch soothed her unraveled nerves.

His hands moved over her back and shoulders, quieting her trembling. She closed her eyes, treasuring the feel of his fingers and the warmth of his body against her own.

When his touch changed from soothing to sensuous, she wasn't quite sure, but it felt as if tiny waves of electric current were coursing over her skin, increasing her awareness of him and his closeness. When his hands stilled, she knew that he felt it, too. His body stiffened against her, she heard the sound of his heartbeat as it began to race, matching the beat of her own.

She lifted her face to look into his eyes, eyes that were bluer and darker than she'd ever seen them before. She raised a trembling hand to touch his cheek and he flinched at her touch. His hands tightened on her shoulders and she didn't know if he would push her away or pull her closer.

I love you. Desperately she wanted to say the words, to tell him that no matter how crazy it sounded she did, in fact, love him. But even to Allison it sounded ludicrous and she knew that Kane would throw the wall back up between them that, for this moment anyway, had been let down.

She'd thought that she'd loved before; her first year out of ballet school she'd been passionate about life and her first experience with a man had led to a short-lived and disappointing relationship. Afterward, she just never seemed to meet the right man. Dance remained her first love, then after her accident, her children at the center.

And now Kane.

The intensity of her feeling for him frightened her. She'd never experienced what she was feeling now. That wild, sweet excitement, the anticipation of wanting a man, of wanting to be made love to and of wanting to be loved.

Cautiously, she moved her fingers down his cheek and the stubble of his beard sent waves of pleasure skimming through her. She touched his jaw, his chin, then moved upward to his lips. He swore softly, closing his eyes as he took hold of her wrist.

"Allison," he said hoarsely and his hot breath fanned the flame of desire running through her. "You're not thinking clearly right now. You've been through a lot tonight, the trauma alone—"

"The only trauma that's going to affect me," she whispered softly, "is if you leave me."

"God, Allison, don't do this, you don't—"

"What I don't want is to be alone tonight," she finished for him, bringing her lips within a whisper of his.

The ache that had been slowly spreading through Kane now turned into a living thing, a wild, primitive creature oblivious to responsibility or duty, a creature that for too long had been denied. But not tonight. Not here, with this woman. Her eyes shimmered with passion, her lips parted, waiting, and even as he told himself to walk away he was pulling her closer, holding her tighter. He breathed in the sweet scent of her, a scent that was hers alone, a scent that drove him over the edge he'd been on since the day he'd met her.

His hands tangled in her hair and the pins tumbled loose, spilling her beautiful mahogany curls down her back. Gently he pulled her head back, keeping his gaze locked with hers as he lowered his mouth. Her hands slid up his chest and her arms wound around his neck.

Their lips met, lightly at first, softly, then suddenly he groaned and ground his mouth against hers, tasting her more deeply and intimately. She met the thrust of his tongue with her own, moving eagerly with the rhythm he set. She made a sound, a soft whimper, and he pulled away then and stared down at her. God, she was beautiful. Her cheeks were flushed with passion, her lips moist and swollen from his kiss.

And she was his. If only for the moment, if only for the night, she belonged to him. He lifted her in his arms, possessively, fiercely, and carried her up the stairs to her bedroom. He stood beside the bed and lowered her to the floor, letting her body slide slowly over his until her stockinged feet touched the floor.

Allison felt Kane's hands circle her waist, then skim slowly up her back. She shivered at his touch and instinctively arched toward him, wanting him to touch her. Need shot through her like a hot, swirling wind, pulling her upward.

"When you walked down the stairs in this dress earlier," he murmured against her temple, "it was all I could do not to throw you over my shoulder and take you to bed. All I thought about tonight was taking it off you."

He undid the top snap and slowly pulled down the zipper,

then slipped the dress off her shoulders. His fingers moved over the top of her exposed arms. His chest constricted as he looked down at her. Silk and lace, that's what she was. A woman he could lose himself to.

That thought had him cursing silently. He tightened his hold on her and pulled her roughly against him. "Do you know how many sleepless nights I've spent thinking of you up here?" he asked hoarsely. "How many times I imagined you like this?"

She leaned into him. "We wasted a lot of nights," she whispered, unbuttoning the first, then the second button of his shirt.

Her hands slipped under the fabric and touched his bare chest. Her fingers were warm and soft and smooth, and when she moved them over his skin he sucked in a breath, fighting back the primal urge to take her immediately and quickly, to simply throw her back on the bed and thrust himself inside her. But she seemed so small beside him, so trusting, and even as he worried that he might hurt her, at the same time her vulnerability excited him as no woman ever had before. He held still, letting her fingers dance magically over him, but when she pressed her lips to the base of his neck something inside him snapped.

Kane's sudden movement startled Allison and she gasped as his arms came around her and lifted her off the floor. He crushed his mouth to hers, parting her lips with a desperation that sent her heart soaring. She wrapped her arms around his neck and pressed herself against him, rubbing the juncture of her thighs against the hard length of his arousal. The pleasure building inside her was unbearable and it screamed for release.

"Kane," she said raggedly, breaking the kiss, but still holding her mouth to his. "Please...please..."

With the last of his control, Kane lowered Allison to the floor again. Placing his hands on her shoulders, he stepped back, then slowly pulled down her dress.

She was perfection. Her breasts, partially covered by a whisper of black lace, were full and round, her skin smooth and soft as white velvet. He tugged her dress over her hips, exposing a sliver of black lace, and knelt in front of her as he pulled the fabric down her legs, revealing the tops of her black stockings. When at last the dress pooled around her feet, she kicked it away. He heard her murmur his name again, urging him to hurry, but he needed to touch her, to taste her, to know every inch of her before he slid into the moist heat of her body.

Need coursed through Allison like a raging river. She bit her lip when Kane pressed his mouth to her stomach and leaned into him, raking her hands through his thick, dark hair. When his hands covered her swollen, tight breasts, she sucked in a slow, deep breath. His fingers kneaded the tight buds of her nipples and pleasure, sharp and painful, ricocheted through her. He unhooked her bra and his mouth replaced his fingers as he tasted her.

Her world was spinning. She'd never thought, never dreamed, that lovemaking could be like this. So completely consuming. That she could hurt this bad and feel this good at the same time. There could never be another man who could do this to her, make her feel this way. She knew that, and while the thought frightened her it gave her a strength and a power she'd never felt before.

He cupped her bottom in his palms and brought her even closer. His mouth and tongue were hot and moist as they moved over her breasts and her stomach, and when he slipped his fingers under the elastic band of lace at her hips and pulled them off Allison felt the heat coil tightly between her legs. A moment later her stockings were gone, too. She stood naked in front of him, trembling with need.

"Kane," she nearly sobbed his name. Her fingernails curved into his shoulders.

The desperate sound of his name sent Kane over the edge. He stood, pulling off his shirt in one swift movement, then dragged her against him again, capturing her mouth with a savage hunger. Her breasts, soft and bare against his own naked chest drove him crazy and he picked her up, muffling her gasp with his mouth as he laid her on the bed. A moment later, his clothes gone, he was beside her, pulling her beneath him.

He looked down at her, saw the passion in her eyes, the need. She made him feel things he didn't want to feel. Powerful, yet weak; savage, yet gentle. He wanted—*needed*—her. Only her.

He held her gaze, struggling with the feelings inside him, but when she raised a hand to him, called his name, he forgot everything else. He knelt over her, wrapped his hands around her knees as he pulled her to him, spreading her legs as he lowered, then sheathed himself in her.

His groan was low and guttural and as he moved, Allison wrapped her legs tightly around him, moving with him, arching upward to take him more fully inside her. Her hair tumbled around her flushed face and her eyes, half closed, were distant and dreamy with intense pleasure. Her head rolled from side to side and at last she opened her eyes fully, gasping as the pleasure overtook her. He watched her climax, then felt the fire overtake him, as well. His own release came with her name on his lips.

Allison stirred in the comfort of Kane's arms and the slight movement had him pulling her tightly against him. It was impossible to know how long they had lain there in each other's arms, but it was long enough for her heart to begin a gradual descent from its rapid-fire beating. She lay her head on his chest and listened to his heartbeat. It was steady and strong. Reassuring. She snuggled closer and slipped one leg over his. He responded by sliding one hand over her hip and the other over her breasts.

"Are you all right?" he asked her in a voice still thick with passion.

She kissed his neck and tasted his damp, salty skin. She realized her own skin was damp, too. "What do you think?" she answered, moving her hands over his chest. "Do you think I'm all right?"

Her voice was as sultry as the night air. When she pressed her lips to his chest, then lightly touched her tongue to his nipple, Kane felt his body respond immediately. "I'd say you are more than all right, lady."

His growl was primal as he rolled suddenly, pulling her beneath him again. Allison gasped at the movement, then moaned softly when he kissed the tip of one breast and flicked the hard peak with his hot tongue. She arched forward, digging her fingers in his hair and pulling him closer. The heat built slowly, but with an intensity that had her writhing beneath him, begging him to end the sweet torture with one breath, then begging him not to stop with the next.

He eased himself into her and began moving slowly, kissing her, nearly withdrawing, then burying himself. Again and again he moved, deeper and harder, bringing her to a height of passion she'd have never thought possible. She clutched at his shoulders, felt the sharp pull of her fingernails over his skin, then cried out, shuddering wildly when at last her release came. He thrust into her again, holding her tightly against him as his own climax racked through his body.

She wrapped her arms and legs around him, holding on to him as the tremors moved from his body into hers. She might not have won the war, she thought dimly, but tonight, if only tonight, she certainly had won the battle.

Eight

Regrets came long before the dim light of dawn cast a hazy glow across the bed covers. Long before he'd opened his eyes and even, for that matter, before he'd closed them. He watched her now, curled against him, her breath slow and warm against his chest, her heartbeat steady, reminding him how fragile life was, how quickly it could be snuffed out. Instinctively he tightened his hold on her, furious that another man had threatened her, furious with himself that he'd almost allowed it to happen. And with that fury came the reality he'd chosen to ignore the previous night, a reality he told himself he'd deal with when the time came.

And the time had come.

He gazed down at her, taking in every detail: her beautiful chestnut hair, wild and sexy from their night of lovemaking, her smooth porcelainlike skin, pale now in the morning light, her lips, wide and full and slightly parted, begging to be kissed....

Desire flamed through his body, sent his heart tripping and his temple pounding. He'd wanted desperately to believe that last night would be enough, that when the morning came he could walk away. But with her body snuggled against his, her breasts burning against his chest and her hands tucked intimately low on his belly, he knew that he hadn't had enough of her, that quite possibly he might not ever have enough of her.

She moved then, stretching slowly against him. He gritted his teeth, determined not to let this go any further. All he had to do was get out of this bed, toss the covers back and get dressed. Not look back.

He stayed where he was.

Cursing himself, Kane laid perfectly still, closing his eyes and drawing in a slow, deep breath as her fingers moved lazily over his stomach, then lower...lower....

With a growl, he pulled her beneath him, watching her eyes widen at his sudden movement. She held his gaze, her eyes a smoky green, her lids heavy with a mixture of sleep and passion. And even as he entered her their eyes stayed locked on each other. Her hands moved up his arms, circling his biceps. Slowly, breathless second by second, he filled her, burying himself within in the liquid fire, letting her consume him and he her.

And then he began to move.

Slowly at first. Her hands tightened on his arms, her fingernails dug into his skin. She moved with him, and when she moistened her bottom lip with her tongue he felt his control slip. He moved faster. Deeper. Took them both higher, then higher still. The need was as strong and as fierce as the night before, but there was something else now, something he did not want to recognize—and it tugged at him, tightened his insides in a way he'd never experienced before.

With each thrust, she took him deeper inside her, but not just physically. It was much more than a joining of bodies; he felt as if she were pulling him into her very soul. The thought terrified him. No woman had made him want like this, need like this, ache like this.

But he was helpless to stop it, powerless to shut off the feelings raging through him. He took her hands, linked her fingers with his and raised her arms over her head, ravaging her mouth as he ravaged her body. Her need was as great as his and she cried out, closing her eyes as her release came. She shuddered beneath him and he groaned deep in his throat, thrusting his head back as a powerful wave of completion surged through his body.

He collapsed on top of her, kissing her hard as he slid his hands down her arms. He rose on his elbows, lifting the weight of his body off of her, and she slid her arms around his shoulders.

"Good morning," she said huskily.

"Morning." He brushed her hair away from her face. Concern etched the corner of his eyes. "How you feeling this morning?"

She smiled softly and slid her hands boldly over his body. "Maybe you should tell me."

He grinned down at her and lowered his lips to her neck. "You feel good here," he murmured, then moved downward to the rise of her breast. "And pretty good here, too."

What Kane was doing to her with his hands and his mouth drove every rational thought from Allison's mind. His lips closed over her hardened nipple and she sucked in a sharp breath, raking her hands through his hair, pulling him closer to her. She wanted only him, needed only him....

Reality intruded with the shrill ring of the phone.

Swearing, Kane rolled quickly away from her. His jaw was tight as he grabbed the receiver. "Yeah."

She watched as he sat on the edge of the bed and snapped the covers off him. "What've you got?"

Icy dread crept through Allison's veins at the crass expletive that burst from Kane. Tension knotted his shoulders as he listened intently for several minutes. When he raised a hand and pulled it through his hair, his muscles expanded and contracted, rippling under skin still flushed from their lovemaking.

"How soon can you get everything to me?" he asked tightly, then after a moment, "Yesterday would be better, but I'll settle for an hour. You still have the fax number I gave you?"

There was a long pause. "Yeah, Sam, I know. I will. Oh—" his voice softened slightly "—give that beautiful wife of yours a kiss for me, will you? On second thought, I'll head out your way when I'm finished here and do it myself."

He hung up the phone, his knuckles white where he still clutched the receiver. Finally he turned to her and she felt a chill seep through her. His face was like granite, and his eyes…his eyes were like shuttered windows, closed for anyone to see into, void of any emotion. The pain cinching around her chest tightened.

"What is it?" Her voice was no more than a weak whisper.

"They've identified the fingerprint. Based on yours and the limo driver's partial description, he's our man."

She drew in a deep breath to steady herself. "And?"

He turned away from her, then reached for his pants beside the bed and pulled them on. "And now we find the bastard."

She knew he'd intentionally avoided her question. "You know what I mean, Kane."

With a heavy sigh, he sat back down on the edge of the bed and looked at her. Though it was only seconds, it seemed like a lifetime before he finally spoke. "His name is Charles Harlan."

Charles Harlan. She could finally put a name to the man who'd turned her life upside down. "And?"

"And what?"

"What's he done?"

She saw the indecision in his eyes. He stared at her, his expression somber. "He's wanted in New York for bank robbery, in Vermont for extortion and in Michigan for murder."

Murder. The word closed around her, sucking the breath from her. *Murder.* "Well," she said with a shaky smile, "he's certainly versatile, isn't he?"

His gaze held steady on hers. "I won't let him get close to you again, Allison."

She pulled the covers up to her chin. "There were two of them. This Charles Harlan and another one driving the car they got away in."

Kane nodded. "Last time he was seen, Harlan had a side-kick named Brad Scott with him. A mindless little punk who couldn't tie his own shoes by himself. He's more of an annoyance than a threat."

"Has he…Harlan…done this sort of thing before?" she asked. "Kidnapping, I mean."

He didn't answer her. An imperceptible tightening of Kane's eyes was the only reaction to her question. Her fingers tightened around the sheet in her hands.

"You told me once you wouldn't hold my hand and you didn't own a pair of kid gloves," she said quietly. "I have to know, Kane."

"Dammit, Allison, we'll get this guy and—"

"Tell me."

He went very still, then drew in a deep breath. "In Michigan."

Michigan. She closed her eyes, letting the icy tremor pass through her before she opened them again. "Where he committed the murder."

Kane nodded tightly.

She wanted him to touch her. To pull her into his arms and tell her again everything would be all right. When he didn't, she knew that he'd retreated behind his job again. There'd be no consolation, no comfort. Nothing that dealt with any emotion beyond what his duty outlined. She pulled up her knees and hugged them to her. "What do we do now?"

Kane moved away from her, picking up his shirt from the floor beside the bed, trying not to think about the feel of her fingers on his chest when she'd taken it off him last night. Trying not to think about last night at all. He couldn't allow himself to. He couldn't.

"Harlan has a younger brother in Chicago, a small-time hood named Nick Harlan who runs a magazine stand. Nick says he hasn't seen his brother for two years, but I'll put a man on him just in case."

He tugged his shirt on. "There's also a girlfriend, a woman named Rhonda Sherman. She's missing right now, but I'll see what I can dig up on her. Other than that, we do what we've always done." He pulled a hand through his hair. "With one exception."

"And what is that?"

"You're not leaving this house."

Allison's eyes narrowed as she slowly lifted her gaze to his. "You know perfectly well that the play is in three days."

"A few days' rescheduling won't matter."

She sat straight, her spine stiff and her shoulders rigid. "I've worked with the kids on this for three months. I wouldn't even change their big day one minute, let alone a few days."

Frustrated, he jammed his hands on his hips and faced her. "Dammit, Allison, I can't protect you if you're running all over the place. Have you forgotten about last night already?"

She stared at him long and hard. "I haven't forgotten one thing about last night," she said quietly.

Her point struck home. Kane held her gaze, and the hurt he saw there in her green eyes cut through him like a knife. He made a move toward her, wanting to slip the covers from her fists, lay beside her and show her he hadn't forgotten, either. That he would never forget. He stopped himself, swearing silently as he stared at the ceiling instead. "Allison," he said softly, "I have a job to do. That's where my head has to be every minute, every second. Your life and the lives of my men depend on me."

The bed dipped when he sat beside her again. He started to reach out to smooth back the hair from her shoulders but stopped himself. He didn't trust himself to stop with a simple touch. "I've lost my objectivity with you, and that's a dangerous thing for a man in my profession."

It was a strange way to tell a woman that he cared for her, but then Kane wasn't exactly what one would call a traditionalist. Allison looked at him, understanding that the danger for him had much more to do with his feelings than it did his profession. He didn't want to care for her, he didn't want to feel. It was easier that way.

Easier for him, at least, she thought angrily. Whether he cared for her or not, when his damn job was finished he'd be gone before the ink was dry on his check. She'd be a fool to hope for more than what their night together had actually been. *A fool.* That's exactly what she was. With capital letters and an exclamation point. She pulled the sheet tighter around her shoulders and forced herself to look straight at him.

"The day after the play I'll take some time off," she said coolly. When he opened his mouth to protest, she cut him off. "It's not up for discussion, Kane. Unless you plan on tying me up or locking me in a closet I'll be at work for the next three days, with or without your consent."

She had the distinct feeling he was seriously considering her alternatives to keep her in the house. His eyes narrowed then and he rose stiffly from the bed.

"Be downstairs in fifteen minutes," he said tightly. "Lessons are now two hours instead of one."

Lifting her chin, she met his hard gaze. "I'll be there."

"No."

"Kane, the play starts in twenty minutes. We need you. You can't say no."

"The hell I can't. Find someone else."

"There is no one else." Allison had to nearly shout over the din of activity buzzing around her. Pint-size woodland fairies, woodsmen, several deer and a frog sprinted about the makeshift stage, all of them excited over the opening of the play. The auditorium was filling up quickly with friends and supporters, and every member of the staff was busy getting everyone in place.

"This costume was built to fit one of our men counselors and he has the flu," she said, straightening the ears of a gray rabbit as it hopped by. "You're the only one who's big enough to fit inside and work the mechanisms."

He wasn't going to do it. He wasn't. Kane stared at the eight-foot mass of cardboard in front of him. It was a tree. Allison wanted him to be a tree. He shook his head again. "I've got extra men here today. I'll get one of them to do it."

With a sigh, Allison folded her arms and faced him. "Kane, what does the tree say to the princess when she gets lost in the enchanted forest?"

He thought for a moment. "Intruder be gone. This is my forest."

Smiling, Allison raised one eyebrow. "Exactly. You've been here every day, watching me work with the kids. No one else knows the lines."

Frowning, he stared down at her. Faint circles rimmed the underside of her eyes and tension knotted her brow. He'd pushed her hard since the night they'd made love. Two-hour lessons in the morning and then he was her shadow for the rest of the day. She'd worked extra hours at the center and went to bed early, but he knew she wasn't sleeping. As he lay there in his own bed, wide-awake, he could hear her moving around in her bedroom above him.

Neither one of them had mentioned the night they'd spent together, but it was there between them. When they touched, when their eyes met. Hell, just being in the same house. The closeness was wearing on him and on her, making them both tense and irritable. And now, to make matters worse, she'd lost one of her main characters for the play.

He felt a small tug on his pants leg and turned his attention downward. It was Courtney. She was playing the part of the princess and she looked beautiful in her frilly white costume. Billy stood beside her, dressed as a woodsman.

"Please, Kane," Courtney said, her blue eyes wide and imploring.

"We can't have a play if you don't," Billy added quietly.

As Kane stared at the children, he realized just how soft he'd become in the past few days. The way they were looking at him right now, he doubted he could deny them anything.

But a tree, for God's sake.

Soft in the brain, that's what he was.

Applause thundered in the tiny standing-room-only auditorium. Allison stood at the back of the stage beside a large cardboard bush, watching with intense pride and pleasure as the cast was introduced to the audience. Faces beaming, each child stepped forward and took a bow.

"Looks like you've got yourself a hit," Kane said from behind her.

Warmed by his compliment, she glanced over her shoulder at him and smiled. "We couldn't have done it without you. If you ever get tired of chasing bad guys, you might consider the theater."

He chuckled. "Something tells me that playing a tree won't exactly get me to Broadway."

She reached up and plucked a silk leaf from his hair. "Everyone has to start somewhere."

She'd made the comment innocently enough, but the undertone hung between them like a sheet of thin glass that would shatter if touched. She couldn't bear that. Not now, not while the exhilaration of the play and the kids' excitement was still humming through her. Those thoughts and those feelings she'd deal with later. In the dark.

She felt him move closer, felt the heat of his body through the cotton blouse she wore. When he leaned close, her pulse began to race.

"You were right," he said softly in her ear. "This play was important. For Billy, for Courtney, for all the kids. To have someone stand up and clap for them. To know that they are important and special, that they're wanted and appreciated." He touched her cheek with his finger and she felt her heart skip. "You gave that to them."

And then that feeling was there again between them, as it had been after the ballet. As if they were the only two people in the room. In the world. Breath held, she turned slowly and looked at him. His gaze touched her tenderly while his thumb skimmed softly over her chin. "You're a very special lady, Allison Elizabeth Westcott."

He leaned down, bringing his lips close to hers, closer—

"Thomas Kane."

They both jumped at the loud call of his name. It was the master of ceremonies, introducing Kane to the audience. Sighing, he grabbed Allison's hand and dragged her out to the center of the stage. Several security men stood at the wall, cheering and whistling loudly. Kane frowned at them, but he couldn't help the smile that tugged at one corner of his mouth. A tree, for crying out loud. He'd have to hear about this for years.

And when the children all surrounded him, hugging his legs and laughing, he decided it would be worth it.

Several minutes later, over cookies and punch and the din of excitement that still vibrated through the auditorium, Allison stepped back from the crowd to catch her breath. Even with the army of security men, Kane still kept a close eye on her, but at the moment he and Billy were surrounded by several well-wishers.

She couldn't help the smile that spread over her lips. He'd only flubbed his lines once, and Billy had helped him through it so the audience hadn't been the wiser. She'd watched the two of them over the past few days and sensed there was a bond growing between them. She felt suddenly guilty, realizing that she'd been so absorbed with her own feelings for Kane she hadn't considered Billy's. The child had been abandoned once. Allison didn't want to think about how he would react when Kane was gone.

Tony moved beside Kane at that moment and whispered something to him. An uneasiness settled over her as she watched the two men, and when Kane looked over at her the uneasiness turned to apprehension. When he realized she was watching him, he quickly averted his gaze and said something to Tony before he walked out of the room. Worried, she started to follow.

"Allison."

She turned back at the sound of her name. It was Helen, the center's director.

"Could I speak with you a moment, please?" the woman asked. "In my office?"

From the expression on Helen's face and the tone in her voice, it was obvious that whatever she had to say couldn't wait.

"I wanted you to hear it from me," Helen said after she quietly closed the door to her office. Allison was well aware of the fact that Tony stood directly outside.

"Hear what?"

"Courtney." Helen glanced toward the office window. It was starting to rain and several drops splashed against the glass.

Courtney. A heavy, sinking feeling settled in the pit of Allison's stomach. *No, not Courtney.*

Allison had stood in this spot too many times, heard too many other children's names, not to know what Helen was telling her.

Courtney was leaving.

"Her parents are here now," Helen explained. "The court's given them permission to take her."

Allison said nothing, just stared blankly at the other woman.

"They've been clean for four months," Helen went on. "They say they love her and want to be the kind of parents she deserves. The grandmother is going to move in with them and make sure they stay clean."

Allison walked to the window and stared out at the parking lot. The concrete was gray and wet. Helen gently touched her arm. "You stay here as long as you need to, dear. I'll tell that nice young man outside that you need a minute alone."

Allison nodded stiffly. At the soft click of the door, she closed her eyes and swallowed down the tears that burned in the back of her throat.

She knew better, dammit. She *knew* better. She'd gotten too close. Cared too much. Pain twisted her stomach and tightened her chest.

She had to be happy for Courtney. She had to believe that everything would work out for her, that she could be with her family and be happy.

Allison realized that the center had been her family for two years. And for two years it had been enough for her. All she'd needed. Now, since she'd fallen in love with Kane, she knew that she needed more. She needed a family of her own. One that couldn't be taken away.

But Kane didn't want that. He was as afraid of loving her as she was of loving these children. What was it he was so afraid of? She wiped at the moisture in her eyes, determined to have it out with him once and for all. If he didn't love her, then she wanted to hear him tell her.

A movement from the parking lot caught her attention and she watched as a tall man stepped out from the passenger's side of a white Jeep. It was Kane. He started to walk away from the car but the driver rolled the window down and called to him. It was a woman, Allison realized. With short blond hair and large, expressive eyes. She was beautiful.

Kane turned and walked back to the woman. She reached out and pulled him down close to her, then said something. Grinning, he leaned close and kissed her. On the lips.

Closing her eyes, Allison drew in a slow, deep breath, then turned and walked back to the party.

Nine

He'd never live long enough to understand women.

Hands tightly gripping the steering wheel, Kane stared at the rain-slick highway ahead of him. Beside him, Allison sat tense and silent. He refused to ask her again if she was all right, knowing that if she said "I'm fine" one more time he just might have to shake the truth out of her.

She wasn't fine, dammit. He just didn't know why. After the play had finished, she'd smiled and laughed with him. She'd been happy. Radiant.

So what had happened?

She'd been talking with Tony and another member of the staff when he'd come back inside from the parking lot. She'd glanced at him, but there'd been no warmth in her eyes, no smile on her lips. She hadn't looked at him once since then, not even when he'd asked her what was wrong.

Traffic slowed as the highway narrowed to two lanes.

Though he hadn't smoked in over six years, he started to reach toward his shirt pocket for a cigarette. He ground his back teeth together when he found nothing there. Frustrated, he flipped the radio on and punched buttons.

Shoulders rigid, Allison glanced sideways at him after he'd run through every button three times. He turned off the radio.

The sky outside was dark and threatening, but the rain had stopped. A wind picked up over the sound, rippling the gray water. He thought of his friend's beach house in Bermuda. Warm ocean, clean sand, blue sky. A month. He'd take off a month after he caught this bastard. What the hell, maybe he'd even take two.

And Allison would still be here. With the kids at the center, making paper sunflowers, going on picnics, planning next year's play...

By the time they pulled into the driveway and parked in the garage, Kane's mood was as foul as the weather. He hadn't even shut off the engine before Allison opened her car door and slid out of the front seat. Swearing under his breath, he turned off the ignition and caught up with her in the hallway outside his bedroom.

"Dammit, Allison. What the hell is wrong with you?" He caught her wrist and pulled her around to face him. He saw the anger flare in her eyes, felt her body tense. For a moment he actually thought she might strike out at him as he'd taught her. Instead, she closed her eyes and sagged against the wall.

"Talk to me," he said gently, placing a hand on either side of her.

Allison opened her eyes and looked at Kane. *Talk to him?* And say what? I love you, but don't worry about it, I'll get over it sometime in the next century. Sighing, she opened her eyes. She couldn't tell him the complete truth, but she could tell him part of it.

"It's Courtney."

"Courtney?" He furrowed his brow. "What about Courtney?"

"Her parents came today and took her back."

She felt him stiffen beside her. "How could they? I thought they were drug addicts."

Allison drew in a deep breath. "They've been in rehab and swear they're clean now. Courtney's grandmother is coming to live with them to make sure they stay that way."

The swear word he uttered was crass and to the point. Fists balled, he pushed away from her and stared at her accusingly. "Why the hell didn't you tell me sooner?"

She felt her own anger start to rise. Damn him, anyway. Why was she suddenly the one feeling guilty? "And what could you have done?"

He looked at her long and hard. "One phone call to the right person and we could have her back tonight."

She not only believed him, for one hope-filled second she even considered it. But she couldn't. She hadn't the right. Slowly, reluctantly, she shook her head.

"Courtney and her parents deserve a chance to put their lives back together again." She sighed. "At least they're trying. Most of the kids at the center, kids like Billy, will never go back to their real families. They'll end up in a foster home."

Eyes narrowed, he stared at her with an intensity that almost frightened her. "Or several."

The raw edge to his words was like a window opening for Allison. Not a door, Kane would never offer that much, but it was enough to understand. She'd seen that look too many times and recognized the pain. "How many were you in, Kane?"

There was an imperceptible tightening of his eyes before he shrugged. "Six. Seven, if you count the one I was in two days."

Seven. A familiar ache settled in her chest. It just wasn't fair. Not for Billy, not for Kane. Not for any child. But then, who ever said life was fair? "Your parents?"

Kane had thought the pain of that memory had died long ago. It surprised him that he was wrong. "Killed in a boating accident when I was seven. I stayed with an elderly aunt for a couple of years, but she couldn't handle the responsibility. The state of Florida took over from there." He shoved his hands in his pockets and almost grinned. "I admit, I was less than gracious about it. I believe the term for children like me was juvenile delinquent."

"You had a right to be angry."

He reached out and tucked a stray curl behind her ear. The strands were soft against his fingers. "I never had anyone like you when it got tough. Your kids at the center are damn lucky to have you."

She shook her head. "I'm the one who's lucky. Every day they teach me something new about life. About challenge and hope and courage. Priorities are a lot clearer through the eyes of a child."

Priorities. His priority was to protect her, to take care of her. How could he do that when all he could think about was how smooth her skin was? How her scent reminded him of wildflowers. Unable to stop himself, he brushed her mouth with his thumb and felt the warm rush of air as she parted her lips. "I'll miss Courtney," he whispered.

Allison closed her eyes, but not before he saw how bright

they were. "Maybe you could check up on her every so often," she said softly. "Discreetly, of course."

He smiled. "Of course."

They stood there, in the gathering darkness, letting the silence of the house surround them. He slid his hand over her shoulder, then down her back, drawing her closer to him. She laid her head against his shoulder and he held her like that, each of them giving comfort to the other.

He'd wanted only to hold her, just for a minute, but his body betrayed him by responding instantly to her closeness. He touched the soft column of her throat and felt the rapid beating of her pulse. And when his mouth replaced his hand, he heard her moan softly, arching her neck back to allow him more room.

He was a fool to think he could keep his hands off her. To think that if he kept his distance he could think more clearly, be more alert. If anything, denying himself had only made him want her more. He brought his mouth to hers, kissed her with a hunger that startled him, even frightened him. He sifted his hands through her hair, drawing her mouth closer and tighter to his. And it still wasn't close enough. It might never be.

She was awash in sensation. The feel of Kane's hard body pressed against hers. His mouth, hot and demanding. His hands, strong and knowing. Insistent. Urgent. She shifted in his arms, desperately needing to be closer. His lips claimed hers again and again, and then her back was against the wall and his hands were on her hips, lifting her, guiding her closer. He murmured her name and moved sensuously against her. She wrapped her arms around him, felt the tension build in her body, between her legs.

God, how she loved him. How she wanted him. Not just here and now, not just in bed, but always. There was something happening between them, something that hadn't happened before. He was touching her in some way he never had. Not with his body, but with his heart.

The image of the blonde in the parking lot suddenly flashed in Allison's mind. The easy way that Kane had kissed her. The fact that he'd never mentioned her. And now he was standing here, she thought, making love to her. She didn't want him this way, not knowing if it was her he was thinking about or that other woman.

She stiffened against him. "Stop, Kane."

His mouth blazed kisses over her jaw. "What?" he murmured against her earlobe.

She pushed at his chest. "I said, stop."

He went still, then lifted his face. She saw the heat of passion in his eyes, and the confusion.

"That woman you were with this afternoon," she said awkwardly.

His brow furrowed. "Woman?"

She felt her impatience rise. "I was in the director's office. I saw you with her in the parking lot."

With a weary sigh, he lifted his face to the ceiling, but not before she saw the guilt in his eyes. The woman *was* someone special to him. She closed her eyes, keeping her pain at bay, knowing she didn't dare release it now.

Her anger, on the other hand, was a different matter.

"Let go of me." She pushed on his chest, but he didn't budge.

He lifted his hand to touch her face. "Allison, it's not what you—"

The sudden and unexpected pain in Kane's hand took him off guard. Allison had a hold on his thumb and was twisting, an easy maneuver he'd shown her that could subdue the biggest man. He swore heatedly and countered by slipping one foot behind her leg and pulling her toward him. She fell backward, then went down, but not before placing a carefully aimed kick mere centimeters from his groin. He let out a whoosh of breath, then fell on her, not only to keep her from scrambling away but to protect himself, as well.

"Dammit, Allison, stop it!"

She couldn't stop. She didn't *want* to stop. She'd held in her anger for too long. The kidnapping. Kane. Courtney. It suddenly became too much. She struggled, furious that he held her down, furious at the knowledge that his strength and his expertise were no match for hers. Chest heaving, she stilled and glared at him. "Get off me."

He tightened his hold on her arms. "Not until you listen to me."

She shook her head. "You told me from the very beginning not to trust anyone, not even you. I wish to God I'd listened to you then, but I sure as hell am not going to listen to you now."

She tried to twist out of his hands, but he held firm. "Allison," he said quietly, "that woman in the parking lot, that was no woman, that was Lainey."

She stilled at his words. "Lainey?"

Suddenly, both Allison and Kane were aware of someone standing over them. Kane looked up and swore. Allison looked up and gasped.

It was the woman from the parking lot. The blonde.

Lainey.

"Hi, kids. I thought I heard someone yell, so I let myself in." Lainey bent down beside them. They both stared at her, too stunned to move. "You know, Allison, what you really need to do here is jerk and twist your arm away from

Kane's, then hook your middle finger over your index and smash him in the eye.''

She smiled at them.

Of all the miserable timing, Kane thought, releasing Allison's arms and rolling off her. Her face was flushed red as she struggled to her knees and stared at the other woman.

"I'm Lainey Randolph." She tossed a dry look to Kane. "You know, the woman who's not a woman."

Kane cast his eyes upward. Heaven save him from females. "Lainey, that's not what I meant."

She arched one delicate brow and folded her arms. "And just what *did* you mean?"

He stood and combed both hands through his hair. "Allison saw me kiss you in the parking lot."

Lainey looked at Allison. "Oh, I see."

Allison couldn't remember when she'd ever been so humiliated. It was bad enough these two had something going on, but to sit and discuss it in front of her as if she weren't there was just too much. How could he be so heartless? Determined to save what was left of her dignity, she straightened her blouse and stood. "If you'll excuse me, I have some work to do."

Lainey understood how deeply a man could make a woman hurt. She laid a gentle hand on her arm. "It's not like that, Allison. Kane are I are old friends. That's all." She looked at him and frowned. "Though after the remark he just made, we may not be anymore."

Allison looked at the woman. She was beautiful. Her hair was a pale blond and cut short to fall in a pixie style around her large brown eyes. Her nose was straight and pert, her skin fair but lightly tanned, as if she spent a lot of time outdoors. Friends, Lainey had said. She and Kane were just old friends. Allison looked down at the rug at her feet, wondering if she could possibly crawl under it.

Still, it didn't explain why the woman was here. Kane didn't strike her as the type to invite old friends over for a visit while he was working.

As if Lainey had read Allison's thoughts, she said, "Kane did tell you I was coming—" she narrowed her eyes as she looked at Kane "—didn't he?"

Kane shifted uncomfortably. "I was going to, but Allison was busy with the play and then I had to help out—"

"He played the part of a tree," Allison interjected.

Amused, Lainey shoved her hands into the pockets of her white slacks. "Really?"

Kane frowned. "No," he admitted, "I didn't get a chance to tell her."

Folding her arms, Allison turned toward Kane. "Tell me now."

He hadn't wanted to tell her like this, in front of Lainey, but now he had no choice. "I've asked Lainey to come in for a couple of days and take over your morning lessons."

Confused, Allison looked from Lainey to Kane. "Why?"

Because you're driving me crazy. Touching you every morning, the feel of your body against mine. God knew they'd probably be in bed right now if Lainey hadn't walked in. He wasn't sure whether to thank the woman or strangle her.

"I need more time at the computer and the phone to trace names and follow leads," he said carefully. "Lainey teaches self-defense to women all over the world. There's no one more qualified to work with you than her."

Allison's eyes were cool as she faced him. "I see."

Dammit, Allison, don't look at me like that. As if he'd just pulled the wings off a butterfly. Didn't she know he was doing it for her own good, because he cared about her? Because he needed to keep her safe?

She turned back to Lainey and offered a weak smile. "I'm sure that you and Kane have a lot to talk about, so if you'll excuse me, I need to get dinner started. I hope chicken is all right with you."

Lainey nodded. "Of course. Thank you."

Shoulders stiff, Allison disappeared into the kitchen. Kane started to follow, then stopped himself, muttering a curse.

Lainey looked in the direction Allison had gone, then back to Kane. "Is there something you'd like to tell me?"

He ran a hand through his hair. "I've already filled you in on the details of the case, but I've got some pictures of Harlan I'd like you to—"

"That's not what I mean, Kane. I'm talking about you and Allison."

Kane met Lainey's curious gaze. "There's nothing to tell."

"Uh-huh." She smiled slowly. "So you two were just looking for a contact lens when I walked in."

His jaw tightened. "That was a misunderstanding."

Lainey controlled the laugh threatening to break loose. This job was going to be more interesting than she'd thought.

"Whatever you say, Kane. I'll just go give Allison a hand in the kitchen. After dinner you can show me those pictures and give me an update."

"Fine."

She moved past him, then stopped and turned around. "Oh, and Kane?"

"What?" he snapped.

She looked at him, one brow raised. "A tree?"

He scowled at her. Laughing, she ducked around the corner. This job was not only going to be more interesting than she'd thought, it was going to be more fun.

"You're not concentrating, Allison."

Sprawled on her back, Allison stared up at Lainey and frowned. It was the third time in less than ten minutes the woman had flipped her neatly onto the mat. "I'm concentrating on how much my rear end hurts."

Smiling, Lainey grabbed a towel off the rec-room floor and dragged it over her damp forehead. "You had that move down perfectly the past two days. Something going on with you today?"

Allison braced herself on one elbow. Something was going on with her, all right. Kane. He'd intentionally avoided her for the past two days, though she knew that he was always close, always watching. She was stuck in this house with a man who'd made love with her and now pretended that she was no more than a business acquaintance. She wanted to choke him. But first she desperately needed his arms around her.

The only bright spot the past two days had been Lainey. It amazed Allison how easily she and the other woman had fallen into a friendship, especially after that embarrassing first meeting. Her cheeks still flamed at the image of Kane wrestling with her on the floor. And yet, at the same time, her body tingled with the memory.

With a heavy sigh, Allison reached for her own towel and wiped at the perspiration on her temple. Lainey might be small, but she was one hell of a self-defense instructor. As tough as she was relentless, the woman demanded attention and refused mediocrity. A female clone of Kane.

"There's nothing going on with me that a few hours by

myself wouldn't cure," Allison complained. "Guards at the front, at the back. Even on the beach. I feel like a fish in a bowl."

Lainey sat down on the mat and combed back her short blond hair with her fingers. "It won't be much longer, Allison. Kane's going to get these guys. Just give him a little time."

"Easy for you to say," Allison said irritably. "You're driving out of here today."

Lainey studied Allison for a moment. "It's more than that, isn't it?" she said quietly.

Allison sat, wincing at the pain in her backside. "What do you mean?"

"Kane."

Allison stilled. "What about Kane?"

"You're in love with him."

It stunned Allison to hear the words out loud. Was she really that transparent? She opened her mouth to deny it, but found that she couldn't. "How could you tell?"

Lainey smiled. "Well, you haven't eaten enough to keep a bird alive, I hear you at all hours of the night, so you're not sleeping, and besides, I recognize the look."

"The look?"

Lainey pulled the towel around her neck. "The same look that used to stare back at me from the mirror."

Allison's fingers tightened on the towel in her hand. "You mean you...and Kane?"

Shaking her head, Lainey crossed her feet and faced Allison. "It was entirely one-sided. Unfortunately for me, my side."

When she realized she was holding her breath, Allison slowly released it. Why should she be surprised? After all, what woman wouldn't be attracted to Kane's rugged masculinity? She'd certainly fallen like a ton of bricks, hadn't she? If she had to get in line, no doubt it would be around the block. "But you...I mean, you and Kane are..."

"Still friends?" Lainey smiled. "I think it hurt him more than me to tell me he didn't feel the same way. But even he knew that what I was feeling was more gratitude than real love."

"Gratitude?"

Lainey drew in a deep breath and wiped the towel over her face. "Kane lived with a foster family next door to mine. He was my older brother's best friend. I've known him since I was nine and he was sixteen." She stared at her hands, then folded them in her lap. "A few years back I...went through a bad time. Kane heard about it and helped me through it. If it wasn't for him, I might not even be here."

And he was still the protector, Allison realized. For Lainey, for her, for anyone in trouble. The protector he'd never had as a child. She hadn't thought it possible to love him more, but a feeling of such profoundness gripped her, of such depth and strength, that her chest ached from the sheer force of it. She wanted desperately to stop the feelings, to make them go away. Maybe then it wouldn't hurt so much when he left.

"Allison," Lainey said gently, "in all the years I've known Kane, I've never once seen him look at a woman the way he looks at you."

Allison's laugh was dry. "You mean like he can't stand to be near me?"

Lainey chuckled. "More like he wants to devour you. Which is exactly why he keeps his distance. Why he called me in to work with you. He's afraid of his feelings for you.

And knowing Kane," she said with a sigh, "he'll fight it to the very end."

No news there, Allison thought.

Lainey leaned forward and her voice dropped to a conspiratorial tone. "But if there's one thing that Kane taught me, it's never give up. He loves you, Allison. You just have to make him realize it."

Make Kane realize that he's in love with me? Allison shook her head. It would be easier to sell summer homes in Antarctica. Still, she thought, no matter what happened, she was thankful she'd met Lainey. "I'm going to miss you."

Lainey grinned at Allison and reached over to give her a hug. "Something tells me we'll be in touch soon. In the meantime, I'll be visiting my cousin in the mountains, about three hours from here. He owns a lodge up there and has several cabins he rents out. When I called him and told him I'd be out here a few days he insisted I come up. I'll leave the number and address if you need to reach me. As soon as you can get away from here, I expect you to come visit me."

Allison returned the hug. "It's a deal."

"Now—" Lainey sprang to her feet "—in the hour I've got left, I'm going to show you how to knock a six-foot-three jerk on his butt."

Smiling, Allison took the hand Lainey offered and stood. This was one lesson she was going to enjoy.

Ten

He was getting nowhere fast.

Jaw tight, Kane drummed his fingers on the polished desk top in Oliver Westcott's study and stared at the files spread out in front of him. Charles Harlan had been careful enough to leave no paper trail for the past two years. No phone, no utilities. Not even a mailing address. It was as if he'd been planning this for a long time. Family members who'd been questioned were less than cooperative and friends had suddenly never heard of the guy. Kane still had a man watching the brother and another man looking for the girlfriend, but so far there'd been no word.

Frustrated, Kane stood and walked to the window overlooking the ocean. Sea gulls soared lazily over a sky that was actually clear, and a few puffy white clouds drifted over the water.

Harlan was out there. Kane knew it. Call it gut instinct,

call it intuition, call it a plain old-fashioned hunch. But he was there. Waiting. He hadn't been scared off by the bungled kidnapping attempt and he hadn't given up. If anything, Kane suspected that Harlan was more determined than ever. Based on his past, tenacity drove the man. He took pride in the fact he'd never been caught, but that pride had made him careless this time. They'd gotten the pictures and a fingerprint. They'd been ready for him.

He could still see the limo pulling away with Allison in it, and that image twisted his stomach into a knot. How could he have lived with himself if Harlan had gotten away with her?

He couldn't have. There would have been no place that Harlan could hide, no place to run that Kane wouldn't have found him. No laws that would keep Kane from seeking his own revenge.

Fists clenched, he turned away from the window and stared at a silver-framed photograph of Allison, sitting on the bookshelf. He picked up the picture and ran his thumb over the smooth, shiny frame. He guessed she was around five or six. Her smile revealed one tooth missing and she was hugging a big white cat. She was adorable. Exactly as he imagined all of her children would be.

He felt a strange ache in his chest at that thought. Allison with a husband, children of her own. He tried to let himself go, to picture himself holding a baby, but he'd spent too many years denying himself that possibility. A kid deserved a real father. Someone who would be there for all the baseball games or dance recitals. Kane's job not only kept him away for weeks at a time, there was always the possibility that he might not come home at all.

And that, more than anything, was the one chance that

Kane could never take. The one pain that he would never risk bringing to a child.

He turned sharply at the sound of the soft knock on the door. "It's open."

Allison stepped into the room and his pulse jumped at the sight of her. Her cheeks were still flushed from her session with Lainey, her eyes bright green against the turquoise leotard and sweatpants she wore. He liked her best this way; with no makeup, her hair tumbling over her bare shoulders. Exactly how she'd looked the morning after they'd made love.

She stared curiously at the picture in his hand. "I thought you might like to know that Lainey is leaving in a few minutes."

"Thanks." He set the picture back down.

Keeping her eyes on him, she moved toward him. He felt his throat go dry and wondered how sweatpants could be so damn sexy.

"Are you feeling safe enough to come out of your haven yet?" she asked in a tone as close to a purr as Kane had ever heard. "Or do you want her to come in here and say goodbye?"

He frowned at her, careful to keep his gaze from drifting down to the swell of her breasts. "I've had a lot of paperwork."

She smiled slowly, knowingly, then sat on the edge of the desk and leaned back. "Of course you have."

He'd seen her sassy and obstinate, angry and despondent. But he'd never seen her so bold. The attitude intrigued him. It also excited him. He looked away from her, determined to keep his mind—and his body—under control. "I'll be out in a minute."

She didn't budge.

Kane ground his back teeth together and moved toward her. He put his hand out and when she placed her hand in his palm he expected her to slide off the desk. Instead, she laced her fingers with his and pulled him closer, tucking his legs between hers.

His hand tightened on hers. She tossed her head back and met his narrowed gaze, daring him to throw her out. He felt the heat of her body, the firm pressure of her thighs against his legs. He looked down at her, saw the rise of her breasts with each breath she took.

There was only so much a man could take.

"I'm not made of stone, Allison. If you don't leave now, you won't be leaving for a long time."

Relief poured through Allison at Kane's words. She'd been terrified to come in here like this, terrified that he'd reject her again. Lainey had made her realize that she couldn't give up on Kane. And Allison's love for Kane had given her courage she would never have dreamed she possessed.

She skimmed a hand up the denim shirt he had on and raised her face to his. "We have to say goodbye to Lainey."

She gasped as he suddenly dragged her against him, spreading her legs as he pulled her to the edge of the desk. "We'll slip a note under the door."

His mouth sought hers with a desperation that made her heart lunge wildly in her chest. She wrapped her arms and legs around him as he pushed her roughly back on the desk. Papers flew to the floor and a silver pencil holder toppled over, spilling its contents. Neither one of them cared. They clung to each other, their mouths and bodies writhing with need. He pulled the neck of her leotard down, exposing her breasts, then fastened his mouth to one taut nipple, laving the sensitive bead with his hot tongue. Allison moaned and tugged impatiently at his denim shirt. With his mouth still at her breast, he tore open the shirt for her. She uttered a cry of delight as she pulled the shirt off his shoulders and raked her fingernails over his heated skin. He was fully aroused, hard and throbbing against her and she reached for his belt buckle, fumbled with the button on his jeans....

The phone rang.

They both swore at the same time. "Let the machine get it," she said between breaths. She saw the hesitation in his eyes and when he brought his lips back to hers she smiled with feminine contentment.

When the phone rang again, he tore his mouth away, cursing with a vengeance, then grabbed the receiver so sharply she thought it might break. "What is it?" he yelled into the receiver.

There was silence at the other end of the line and Kane almost slammed down the receiver. Before he could, a hesitant feminine voice said, "Is this Kane...Thomas Kane?"

He had to strain to hear the voice on the other end. It was no more than a whisper. A frightened whisper.

"Yes, I'm Kane."

Silence again.

"Who is this?" he asked gently.

"Rhonda," she answered after a moment. "Rhonda Sherman."

Harlan's girlfriend.

"Your friend left this number with my mother in Chicago. She thought I should call you."

On the other end of the line, Kane heard a horn honking and the rush of traffic. A pay phone. He glanced up at Allison. Her eyes were heavy lidded, her lips still wet from his kiss. She'd already pulled her leotard back up to cover her breasts, but he could clearly see the outline of her hard nipples through the thin fabric. He gripped the receiver so tightly the plastic cracked in his hand.

"Are you there?" she asked nervously.

"Yes, yes. I'm here. Talk to me."

Her voice lowered. "I can't. Not here. Meet me at the hamburger stand at Sixth and Chapman. I—" she paused "—I know where you can find Charlie."

"I'll be there in twenty minutes. Tell me—"

She hung up. Kane stared at the receiver in his hand. *Rhonda.* She was here, in Seattle. And she sounded scared. People talked when they were frightened.

Arms tightly folded, Allison stood beside the desk. "Where are you going?" she asked quietly.

He hung up the phone and started to button his shirt before he realized he had no buttons. He looked at Allison with surprise and saw the blush color her cheeks. The wild abandon of their near lovemaking brought a renewed surge of desire pounding through his blood. He had to get out of here now, before he lost control completely.

"I have a lead to follow up on," he said tersely, moving toward the door. "Tell Lainey to leave me a number where I can reach her and I'll call her later."

Allison fought back the panic rising in her. She couldn't let him leave her like this. She needed him; not just physically, she also needed the comfort of knowing he was close by. Following him to the door, she laid a hand on his arm when he reached for the knob. "Let me go with you."

He shook his head. "It's safer here."

"Kane," she pleaded, "I'm going crazy in this house." *I'm going crazy without you.*

He turned to look at her, but his hand stayed on the doorknob. "Allison," he said quietly. "Your father hired me to protect you. You've got to give me the space to do my job.''

In other words, leave me alone. Hurt sliced through her clear to the bone. Maybe she'd been wrong. Maybe for Kane their relationship was just physical. She released his arm and stepped back. "Of course."

He started to say something, to move toward her, but he didn't. He simply opened the door and left, closing it quietly behind him.

She stared at the door, determined to give him all the space he wanted and then some.

It was hot under the thick cotton blanket. Hot and stuffy. Allison lay on the back seat floor of Lainey's car, her knees tucked tightly to her. Her foot had fallen asleep and she had a cramp in her left leg, but she didn't dare move. She barely dared to breathe.

They'd been gone about an hour, Allison guessed, give or take a few minutes. Enough time to put some serious distance between herself and her father's house. Between her and Kane.

The only problem was, Lainey didn't know Allison was back here. And Allison didn't dare spring it on Lainey while they were driving down the road at sixty miles an hour. That meant she had two more hours to go, squashed back here like a sardine.

She'd been impulsive, but she didn't care. Kane had told her he needed space. Well, so did she. She couldn't even go out and get the mail without two sets of eyes watching her. And even though she'd been impulsive, she hadn't been foolish. No one had seen her sneak into Lainey's car and bury herself under the blanket. And if no one knew where she was, then no one could find her.

Including Kane.

The car hit a bump then and Allison stifled a grunt. The cramp in her leg was worse and both feet were asleep now.

"You know, Allison, you really should come up out of there before you suffocate."

Damn. She'd been found out. Embarrassed, but beyond caring, Allison tossed back the blanket and gulped in a lungful of air. Lainey glanced over her shoulder, then shook her head as she pulled the car into the slow lane. "I was wondering how long you'd survive back there."

Allison slowly unfolded her stiff limbs, groaning from the effort it cost her. "How did you know I was back here?"

Lainey chuckled. "The first thing I teach in self-defense is check your back seat. Since I knew I didn't have a pair of white flats, my next guess was a stowaway."

"And you let me come with you?"

"You're a big girl. I figured if you wanted to get out of there that badly, then that was your decision."

"Thanks, Lainey." With a sigh, Allison folded her sore body over the front seat and sat. "I hope this won't cause any trouble for you."

"I've been in trouble before and hey, if anyone asks, I never knew you were back there."

"I did leave him a note," Allison explained. "I just forgot to mention where I'd be."

They rode in silence for a few minutes and Allison appreciated the fact that Lainey didn't ask any questions. Maybe later they'd talk— In fact, Allison was sure they would. After all, the woman deserved some kind of an explanation. But for now, Allison intended to enjoy her independence. She settled herself comfortably into the front seat and laid her head back against the cushioned headrest. No leash. No watchdog. Just pure, sweet, blissful freedom.

"He will find you, you know," Lainey finally said. "He's very good at what he does."

Allison looked at Lainey. "The best."

"He's also going to be furious."

Allison nodded. "He is, isn't he?"

Both women smiled at each other.

When Kane pulled into the Westcott estate several hours later, he was wound up tighter than the proverbial watch spring. He'd waited two hours for Rhonda, but she hadn't shown. Another dead end.

He considered the possibility that her call had been a setup. An attempt to lure him away from Allison. But the woman had truly been afraid. He'd heard it in her voice, and Kane was certain the call had been real. Something— or someone—had kept Rhonda from that meeting. All he could do now was wait for her to call again.

But they were getting close. Of that he was certain. Damn close.

He parked Allison's car in the driveway and stared at the seat beside him. It was piled high with an assortment of paper flowers and brightly colored pictures that said "I love you" and "I miss you" and "Please come back soon." While he was out, and since he'd been so close, he'd stopped by the center. He hadn't planned on staying more than a minute, but a video game of Street Racer with Billy had somehow turned into a tournament of champions and before he knew it, an hour had gone by.

And then, when he'd started to leave, the look of disappointment on Billy's face had been like a cinch around Kane's chest. He knew that look, and he also knew what it felt like to be left alone with strangers. With family that really wasn't family.

It felt lonely. And empty.

So he'd stayed another hour.

With a heavy sigh, Kane gathered up the gifts, hoping they would soften Allison's anger when she found out he'd gone to the center without her. Her image had burned in his mind all day. The whisper-soft touch of her lips on his neck, the rasp of her fingernails on his skin. Unexpected, the scent of her would drift to him and he'd think of how soft her skin was, how smooth her throat. How tight she fit around him when he slid into her. It was driving him crazy. *She* was driving him crazy.

No woman had ever made him feel the way she did. Not physically, and certainly not emotionally. A look, a touch, the sound of his name on her lips as he moved inside her. She made him feel whole. She made him feel real.

And that scared the hell out of him more than anything. Because if he took the risk and he lost, it would be like losing his last breath of air.

Arms laden with the children's gifts, Kane strode up the walk, nodding to the day watch as he let himself in the front door. The house was quiet inside. He listened for the sound of music, which Allison normally would have on, but there was none.

She was probably out back, he decided and deposited the presents on the dining-room table. He knew she enjoyed working in the garden on nice days. He stuck his head out and questioned the guard out back. He hadn't seen her all day.

"Allison?"

No answer.

It was too damn quiet.

A strange mixture of panic and fear swept over him and he quickly moved up the stairs. Reaching under his jacket, he called her name again, then pulled his revolver out from the holster under his jacket. Heart pounding, he went into her bedroom first, then made a sweep of the rest of the rooms. Everything was in order, except for Allison.

He was on his way to question the men outside when he saw the note on the floor beside the dining-room table. He must have knocked it off when he'd set down the gifts.

He picked it up and read.

Eyes narrowed, jaw tight, Kane stormed to the front door and bellowed.

By late afternoon the cabin was aired out, the car unloaded and the groceries put away. Lainey talked on the phone with her cousin, while Allison, dressed in Lainey's cotton robe, sat in front of the fireplace. Her skin was still damp from the quick shower she'd taken. She leaned closer to the fire, letting the flames warm her as she combed the tangles from her wet hair. When they'd stopped at the market in town, Allison had picked up a toothbrush and a few toiletries. She hadn't taken the time this morning to pack a bag, but she had brought money.

The smell of wood smoke and pine trees filled the one-room cabin. It was small but cozy, with an overstuffed sofa that made into a bed, one wooden rocker and a maple dining-room table with four chairs. The tiny bathroom had a tub with a hand-held shower. There was no TV, no stereo system, no garbage disposal or dishwasher.

And the best part of all—no guards.

Allison stared at the wavering flames, wondering how Kane was taking the news of her desertion. Not very well, she assumed. But that was his problem. She'd left him a note, and as far as she was concerned that was enough. Maybe he would find her here, and maybe he wouldn't. She was done caring about what Thomas Kane did or didn't do, what he did or didn't like.

Lainey hung up the phone and grabbed two peaches before flopping herself down on the sofa. "We've got a date tonight."

Allison's fingers stilled on her wet hair. "What?"

She tossed a peach to Allison. "My cousin. He insists on taking us to dinner at the lodge in an hour."

"But I can't. He doesn't even know me. I haven't anything to wear and—"

Lainey brushed off the fruit in her hand, then took a bite. "The slacks you wore here are fine."

"I don't want to be a bother," Allison protested.

"My cousin is a hunk." Lainey wiggled her finely arched brows. "And single."

Allison raised her eyes to the ceiling and shook her head. "I'm here to get away from men, thank you very much."

"If you don't come, then I can't go," Lainey insisted. "It's one thing to bring you up here with me, but another to leave you alone. Kane would never forgive me that."

Allison took an indignant bite of her peach. "What Kane will or won't forgive doesn't concern me in the least."

"Well, it does me." Lainey pulled up the sleeves of her sweatshirt. "He might be pigheaded and stubborn, but he's a good friend. I'm already pushing the limits of trust in our friendship."

Allison sighed. "I'm sorry, Lainey. I obviously wasn't thinking when I dragged you into this."

"You didn't drag me into anything. I knew you were hiding in the back seat of my car, remember?" She smiled. "But if you tell anyone, I'll deny it."

Lainey started to take another bite of her fruit, then stopped suddenly. She tilted her head, listening. "Good Lord, he's better than I thought."

"Who?"

"You might want to get dressed." Lainey stood and went into the kitchen. She tossed her peach pit into the trash and brushed off her hands.

"But you said we had an hour."

Lainey folded her arms and stood by the kitchen counter. "Not anymore we don't."

The cabin door burst open. The walls reverberated with the force and the windows rattled.

Kane stood in the doorway. He *filled* the doorway. His face was tight with fury, his eyes dark and fierce. Allison had certainly expected him to be angry, but she'd never expected the rage she was suddenly faced with. Knees trembling, she slowly stood.

"Hi, Kane," Lainey said cheerfully.

"You—" he addressed Lainey, but did not look at her. "I'll talk to you later. And you—" his eyes narrowed sharply as he stared at Allison "—I'll talk to now."

"I was just going to get some firewood." Lainey reached for her jacket.

"You stay right there." Where Allison found her voice she wasn't sure, but despite the shaking she felt inside she sounded reasonably calm. "This is your cabin and Kane is not going to chase you out."

"Don't mess with me, Allison," Kane threatened, taking a step into the cabin.

She pulled her robe tightly around her. "I wouldn't dream of it. In fact, I wouldn't want to touch you with a ten-foot pole."

His jaw tightened. "Get in the car. We're going back."

"I'm not going anywhere. I'm here as Lainey's guest and I'm staying."

Kane had never forced a woman to do anything in his life. But no woman had ever mattered to him like Allison. Nor had any woman ever made him so angry. He wanted to throw something, smash something. He struggled to control the fury inside him. It had taken him thirty long, agonizing minutes to trace them down and three more hours on the road to get here. He was in no mood for this.

He'd ask nice. Then he'd pick her up and carry her. "Get in the car," he said tightly. "Please."

"No."

He took another step into the room, trying not to notice the way the firelight behind her outlined her body through the thin robe she had on, trying not to notice the way her damp hair fell in a wild mass of curls around her face. He knew the silken feel of those thick tresses over his skin, in his fingers, and that knowledge had him clenching his hands.

"This is no game, Allison."

"Game?" She felt her own anger rising. "My life has been threatened, I have a home I can't go to and a job I can't work at. I can't even walk outside without three sets of eyes watching my every move." It was her taking a step toward him now. "Nobody, I repeat, *nobody,* knows better than me this is no game."

No more than two feet apart, they faced each other. Her arms were folded, his hands were balled into fists. He was too angry to speak, she was too angry to be quiet.

"You told me you wanted space to do your job, so I gave it to you. As far as Harlan knows, I'm still sitting cozy in my father's house. No one saw me leave and no one knows I'm here. I'm a hell of a lot safer here, physically and emotionally, and I guarantee you—'' she leveled her gaze with his ''—I'm a hell of a lot happier.''

He winced under the force of the verbal jab. He was supposed to protect her, keep her from harm. Instead, he'd taken her to bed, then dismissed her as if it had meant nothing to him.

''Allison...'' He started to reach for her, then realized they weren't alone. He turned to Lainey, who was watching with great interest. He frowned at her. She smiled.

''Don't mind me,'' she said, gesturing him to continue.

''Lainey,'' he threatened.

Sighing, she shrugged into her jacket. ''Best show of the year and I have to miss it.''

''Just a minute.'' Allison put out a hand to stop Lainey. ''I'm coming with you.''

Lainey shook her head apologetically. ''Sorry, Allison. I'm afraid you're on your own.'' She gathered up her purse and then, as an afterthought, picked up her overnight bag. ''I think I'll stay at the lodge tonight. The water is hotter and the beds softer. And it's probably a little quieter, too,'' she added, tossing them a wave as she opened the door. ''Have fun, kids.''

''But—''

Lainey closed the door, cutting off Allison's protest. Frowning, she turned back to Kane. ''You had no right to chase her out of here.''

''She made her own decision. And a wise one at that.''

''I'm not going back with you, Kane.''

He was tired of arguing. ''Fine. I don't feel like a three-hour drive back anyway. We'll stay here for the night.''

''We? Where are you getting we? There is no we. I came here to get away from you.''

Her words cut him like a jagged knife. He deserved them, but they hurt nonetheless. "Pretend I'm not here."

Pretend he wasn't here? Her senses were on overload with the man. The light from the fire danced blue in his eyes and cast rugged shadows across his handsome face. Even scowling he was devastating, perhaps more so. Like a wild creature. Fearsome and uncivilized. He brought that trait to bed with him, she realized and cursed the rush of excitement that skittered over her skin.

It was too much. Wanting him. Needing him. Loving him. And knowing that he would leave her the minute Harlan was found. She turned her back to him and stared at the fire, wondering how such a beautifully romantic setting with the man she loved could seem so desolate and lonely.

"You're much better at pretending than I am, Kane," she said quietly. "Give me some time, though. With a little practice, I just may learn to be as cold and unfeeling as you."

There was silence behind her. A long, taut silence broken only by a squirrel's chatter outside the cabin. She heard the creak of the sofa, felt the tension in the room increase. His hand closed around her arm with bruising force. Her breath held. She knew he was capable of violence and wondered briefly if she'd pushed him too far, but she was beyond caring.

When he pulled her around to face him his eyes glittered with barely contained anger. It was different than when he'd first walked into the room. It went deeper, was more powerful. And more frightening.

"Unfeeling?" The word was a ragged whisper on his lips. "Lady, I wish to God I didn't feel. Then maybe I wouldn't spend every minute of every day thinking about how damn good you feel in my arms and under my body.

Maybe I wouldn't think about how the touch of your hands on my skin arouses me to the point of sheer agony." His hand tightened painfully on her arm. "And maybe I wouldn't think about how it's killing me, bit by bit, every time I deny myself what I know we both want."

She let out a small sound of protest when he pulled her against him. His body was rigid, like tightly coiled wire. "When I got back to the house and couldn't find you I nearly went crazy. If I hadn't figured out you were with Lainey, I probably would have torn every room apart with my bare hands.

"Unfeeling," he said again and his laugh was dry, sarcastic. "I haven't had a rational, much less coherent thought in days, knowing that you were there, no more than a few feet from me, and I couldn't have you."

He pulled her closer still. "But not tonight, Allison," he said roughly. "Tonight it's just you and me. Nothing else and no one else. Tell me that you want that, that you need that, as much as I do. If you can't, then stop me now, while you still can, while I still have a thread of control still holding me together."

Her heart was hammering wildly in her chest. Though his words were hardly an admission of love, they were more than he'd ever given her before. Perhaps more than he'd ever give her again.

She looked up at him and met the hard glint of his eyes. "Kane, would you please stop talking and kiss me?"

Eleven

His crushing embrace lifted her off the floor and his mouth caught hers with a fierce passion. Allison's heart soared as she wrapped her arms around Kane's neck. It had always been this way with them, the wild, almost savage need they felt for each other. His tongue thrust insistently, rhythmically, and she met him fully, drawing him deeper into her, stroking him, teasing him. Her fingers raked through his hair and came around to tightly clasp his jaw. Closer. She wanted him closer.

She tasted of peaches and passion. He thought he might go crazy with the need exploding through him right now. *Crazy.* He *was* crazy. Crazy to feel her beneath him, to feel the hot, tight glove of her body as he slid into her. There was no other word to describe the sweet torment he felt, no other word to explain why he couldn't stay away, why even now, holding her against him, it still wasn't enough.

Her back was hot from the fire, but it was nothing compared to the inferno roaring through him right now. He
cupped her rear end in his palms and fitted her against his
arousal, pressing the hard length of himself into the softness
between her legs. He felt, more than heard, the moan from
deep in her throat and the sound drove him wild.

Lowering them both to the floor, he stretched out along-
side her, kissing her as his hands moved over her long, lithe
body. She was beautiful. So incredibly beautiful. Her hair
spread out around her face like an exquisite fan of shimmering copper. Her face was flushed from their kiss, her
lips moist and parted. This is what he dreamed of every
night, what possessed him in his waking hours. Allison.
Like no other woman ever had. Like no other woman ever
would again.

Desire danced in her eyes, beckoning him. He traced the
outline of her body with his hand. Over her shoulder, up
the slender column of her lovely white neck. Then slowly
down, following the vee of her robe, where skin met cotton.
When he slipped his fingers under the fabric she gasped.
When he caressed the soft swell of her breast she moaned.
And when his lips closed over the thin fabric and sucked
on her already hard nipple she cried out.

Allison felt herself trembling under Kane's slow but pre-
cise attention. *Hurry,* she wanted to scream. Before she
burst into flames. She felt light-headed, dizzy, and when he
tugged open the belt of her robe, pushing the cotton aside
as he took her into his mouth, she was sure she *had* burst
into flames.

She ran her hands over his shoulders, felt the rippling
cords of his muscles as he shifted his attention to her other
breast. Pleasure rocketed through her, had her arching up
to meet him, wanting him to take her more deeply into him.

He obliged, laving her hard, swollen nipple with his hot tongue.

"Kane," she sobbed his name. "Please, I can't stand it."

He raised himself over her, straddling her, smiling softly as he gazed down at her. She was naked to him, except for a thin strip of silk panties. As if he had all the time in the world, he casually unbuttoned his shirt and pulled it off. "This time we go slow, Allison. I want to watch your eyes as I touch you here...." His knuckle brushed her nipple and she drew in a sharp breath. "And here." His palm cupped her breast. "And here."

His hand circled the juncture of her thighs and when he slipped one finger under the elastic of her underwear she bit her lower lip. "No," she said raggedly.

"Yes."

Two fingers.

She gasped. "Damn you."

His chuckle was husky and erotic.

He whispered to her what he wanted to do to her and she whispered yes. *Yes.*

As he promised, he took his time. His hands moved over her like hot liquid satin. His kisses were deep and long and hard. His teeth bit and nipped, his lips teased. He brought her to the tip of a towering cliff where the rock was slowly breaking away under her feet. She had nothing but the sky to reach for, to hang on to.

Through a dim haze, she glanced up at him as he stood to slip off his jeans. Firelight danced over his glistening bare skin. He was so beautiful. So incredibly magnificent.

And so ready.

He knelt over her, watching her intently as he spread her legs. The dark blue of his irises darkened to midnight when he entered her, and as he began to move she saw flames in his eyes. The same flames that licked at her body and burned her skin. She rose to meet him, her breathing fast and furious, her heart pounding fiercely. His hands moved down her thighs and hooked her legs around him.

"Kane," she cried out. *"Kane."*

He pulled her closer, moved deeper inside her. Her nipples brushed his hair-covered chest with every thrust. Sensation after sensation swirled through her, until the cliff held but one simple stone beneath her feet.

And when that fell away, she screamed.

Kane fell with her, his release an explosion of need and want, of passion and desire.

Of love.

Several long seconds—or was it minutes?—passed before either one of them could move. It was like the mists of a dream just between night and waking. In the space between real and unreal. The fire crackled beside them. A cuckoo clock chirped out the hour. A mild wind sang through the tall pines outside. There was no one named Harlan in this place, no one watching. It felt like forever.

Kane eased himself from Allison, but could not bring himself to withdraw. He needed this time, this moment, as desperately as he'd needed the release. He kissed her shoulder, tasted the salt on her skin, then nuzzled a spot beneath her earlobe. With a sigh, she wound her arms tightly around him.

"If I'd known this would happen, I would have taken off days ago," she murmured softly.

"If I'd known—" he skimmed his lips over her ear "—I would have sent you myself."

Her eyes widened when he moved deeper inside her.

"Kane?"

"Hmm?"

He moved again, slowly, sensuously. She had to think a moment, to remember what it was she wanted to say. "I...I'm sorry if I worried you."

He lifted his head and looked at her. His eyes were softer now, less fierce. "I nearly ripped the head off the gate watch. He's the one you'll need to say you're sorry to."

She closed her eyes and nodded. "When we get home tonight I'll—"

"Tomorrow."

Surprised, she stared at him. "You mean, we can stay? Here? Tonight?"

Her skin was still flushed with passion, her lips still swollen. The entire secret service couldn't drag him out of here. "I thought we might continue your lessons up here."

"Oh, really?" Her hand snaked shamelessly up his leg.

"Uh-huh." Slowly, he lowered his mouth to hers. "There's still a few moves we haven't covered yet."

"Kane, this is unnatural."

"It is not."

"It's disgusting, too."

"You'll get used to it."

"I don't want to get used to it. It's got to hurt."

Kane took Allison's hand and guided her. "Stop being a baby and just do it."

"Oh, all right, already."

She took a deep breath and shoved the hook through the worm.

Grimacing, Allison held the fishing pole away from her and watched the wiggling worm dangle in midair.

"Yuk." She shivered and looked away.

Laughing, Kane cast Allison's line for her, then set about

baiting his own hook. The lake was smooth as glass, but at six in the morning it was also freezing cold. The sky was slowly fading from dark gray to pale blue and the pine trees were alive with the song of birds and the chattering of squirrels. Smoke curled from the cabin's chimney and the rustic scent mingled with the sweet smell of pine.

Allison shivered through the heavy jacket Kane had found for her when he discovered the fishing gear in a closet. "Why is it necessary to do this at such an ungodly hour?"

"That's when fish are hungry." Kane cast his own line out. "Besides—" he leaned close and the warmth of his breath whispered over her lips "—we were awake anyway, remember?"

As if she could forget. They'd fallen asleep in each other's arms and hadn't slept long before she'd felt the sensuous brush of his lips on her shoulder and the electrifying touch of his hands moving over her hips. After he'd made love to her, he'd asked her if she wanted to do something she'd never done before. She hadn't realized at the time he had *fishing* in mind.

For the next few minutes they sat in silence at the edge of the lake, staring at their unmoving lines. Neither one of them had mentioned Harlan, but he was here with them, on both their minds. Kane had slept with his gun close by and several times, when the cabin creaked or a twig cracked outside, his body had gone tense. And yet she knew that Kane felt safe here or he never would have stayed. He was more relaxed than she'd ever seen him and they hadn't even argued once. A miracle.

She allowed herself the luxury of watching him as he sat comfortably on the edge of the lake with his arm resting casually on one bent knee. The beginnings of a beard darkened his lower face, and his hair tumbled haphazardly over his forehead. Her insides warmed and fluttered as she remembered how she'd begged him to make love to her while she'd combed her fingers through that thick, dark hair. She smiled then, also remembering that before the night was through he himself had begged.

Her gaze roamed like loving hands over his body, admiring the snug jeans and strong hands. Hands that were gentle and tender one minute, then fierce and demanding the next. She noticed a small jagged scar on his temple and wondered how he'd got it.

She knew so little about him. Who he was. What he liked. What he'd done. Things a woman wants to know about the man she loves.

"Lainey told me you and her brother are friends." A statement, rather than question. He could respond or not.

He was quiet for a moment and then, as if remembering, he smiled slowly. "I'd been with a foster family for a year when Steve moved in next door. I was jealous of any kid who had a real family, and I didn't need much of a reason to pick a fight. Steve was smaller than me at the time, but he was also a brown belt. He kicked my butt. I was like a shadow after that, begging him to teach me what he knew."

Allison smiled. It was hard to imagine Kane asking anyone for anything. "Lainey also told me that you helped her through a bad time."

Kane's smile faded and a darkness fell over his features. A mixture of anger and sadness. The sound of the breeze through the treetops was like a distant waterfall, and the call of a lone bird from across the lake echoed mournfully.

"Five years ago Lainey was raped."

Raped. Every woman's nightmare. A tightness cinched Allison's chest. She looked across the shimmering lake, wondering how, in a world so beautiful, there could be so much ugliness.

"It was a tough time for the family. Her parents were devastated and Steve wanted to kill the guy."

"They knew who did it?"

"We knew, all right. But he was the police chief's son. It was his word against Lainey's. The trial was a joke. Lainey was humiliated and the bastard went scot-free." Allison saw Kane's fingers tighten on his fishing pole. "After the trial, she wouldn't come out of her room and her parents were scared she might do something."

"And you?" Allison asked.

"I was in the army at the time, in the Middle East. When Steve called I came back on a temporary leave."

Kane looked at her, but she felt as if he were seeing through her. "I could have killed the guy easily. With the training I'd had, no one ever would have known it wasn't an accident."

Allison felt a chill seep through her at the hard glint that sharpened Kane's eyes. "But you didn't," she said quietly.

"I went to Lainey first and told her. She hadn't talked for days and I didn't know if she even understood what I said. When I turned to leave she said one word, then started to cry." He glanced out over the lake. "She said 'no.'"

Allison wondered briefly what she would have said. She prayed silently she would never know.

Kane pulled gently on his fishing line. Ripples skimmed across the water. "I stayed with her for a month. We talked. Took a lot of walks. I worked on some self-defense moves with her. For Lainey, that was the turning point."

"And now she teaches other women."

He nodded. "She's a fourth-degree black belt now." She

saw the pride in his eyes when he smiled. "Even I have to watch myself around her."

Allison ignored the tug on her fishing pole. "She told me she fell in love with you."

He glanced quickly away. "Did she tell you I asked her to marry me?"

Marry her? Stunned, she simply stared at him, hating the pang of jealousy that shot through her.

Kane looked at Allison. "No, I guess she didn't." He sighed. "She was a lot wiser than me and told me no. She knew I had asked her for all the wrong reasons."

"But you did...I mean, you told me you were married."

Kane pulled up his line and the hook was empty. Frowning, he reached for another worm in the bait box. "I was. A year after Lainey went to Japan to study martial arts I was stationed in Georgia. I met a woman there named Sandy and fell in lust. Four months after we were married I was assigned to a desert-warfare training center in the middle of the Mojave. That place gave new dimension to the word 'hellhole.'"

Kane hooked the worm and cast his line again. "Two months later I came home and found my loving wife in bed with another man—the colonel who'd transferred me."

She wanted to reach out to Kane, to touch him, but when he turned away from her she sensed that he was embarrassed he'd suddenly told her so much.

A strong, sudden jerk on her line caught her attention and she gasped. Kane grabbed for the pole.

"Keep the line tight!" he shouted. "Don't let it get away!"

Kane watched the excitement light Allison's face as she struggled with the pole. She was laughing and yelling with the delight of a child catching her first fish. He laughed with her, shouting instructions while he scrambled to net the wiggling trout she pulled out of the water. It struck him he couldn't remember the last time he'd laughed like this. It had been too long, he realized. Much too long.

And he also realized, with a force that nearly had him sitting back down again, that he loved Allison.

He loved her. *He loved her.* He felt as if he'd been cold-cocked. He turned slowly, net still in his hand and stared at her. Her eyes were bright with exhilaration and as green as the pine trees surrounding them. Her cheeks were flushed with excitement. She was the most incredible, beautiful woman he'd ever met.

Last night she'd told him he was unfeeling. God, if she only knew. Feelings were tearing him apart, clawing at his insides. Feelings he'd thought he'd put behind him after losing his parents and moving from one family to another. It was easier and less painful not to feel. He couldn't change now and allow himself to care like this, to love her. Because if he did, it would kill him when he lost her.

And he *would* lose her. Maybe not now, but how long would it be before she wanted marriage and babies? A husband with an eight-to-five job that allowed him to be home on weekends for barbecues and Little League?

It wasn't enough to love her. A woman like Allison deserved more than that. Much more than he could ever give.

He laid the net down and moved close to her, then gently touched her face with his fingertips. This was how he wanted to remember her. With her eyes bright and eager and her skin aglow with love. Love for him.

He ran his fingers over the smooth line of her jaw, then traced the outline of her lips with his thumb. Her thick lashes fluttered down when he lowered his mouth and he felt her tremble beneath him when he softly pressed his lips to hers.

No one had ever kissed her like this, Allison thought dimly. So tenderly. So sweet. With such longing that her chest ached. And she knew, as only a woman could know, that he was kissing her goodbye.

The pain was too deep and too sharp to acknowledge it. Instead, she felt herself go numb. She would not hold him to her with tears or arguments. He had to love her enough to take the risk. He had to love her as much as she loved him.

Obviously, he did not.

She wouldn't think about him leaving. Not now. There'd be plenty of time later. When she was alone. Forcing a smile, she moved away from him. "I think we better get back now."

While Allison gathered up the poles, Kane clipped the hook from the fish and dumped it into a bucket. When he bent to close up the tackle box, she stared at the silvery trout for a long moment, then quietly picked up the bucket and stepped to the edge of the lake. Her throat burned as she dumped the fish back into the water and watched it swim away.

They were both quiet on the walk back. Inside the cabin Allison got her things together, while Kane called the house and checked in with his men.

She was arranging the pillows on the sofa when he hung up the phone. He stared at her, his expression a mixture of astonishment and disbelief.

"What is it?" she asked hesitantly.

"Harlan." He ran a hand through his hair and let out a

loud breath. "His girlfriend got scared and tipped off the police. They picked up him, and his buddy, Brad Scott, early this morning."

"Take your time, Miss Westcott," Detective Fandino said quietly to Allison. "They can't see or hear you, and we want you to be sure."

Arms folded tightly in front of her, Allison drew in a deep breath and looked at the five men lined up on the other side of the one-way glass. A voice from an overhead speaker instructed each man to step forward and turn first to the left, then the right. Beside her, Allison felt the tension radiate from Kane as he stared at the men.

By the time the fourth man stepped forward, Allison felt as if her stomach had been turned inside out. They all looked the same to her. Every man had dark hair, similar facial features and roughly the same body build: tall, with broad shoulders and a wide neck.

"I never actually saw his face," Allison said as the fifth man was called forward. "He never even turned around. I just saw his—"

Eyes.

The fifth man. He stepped forward and stared blankly at her. His eyes. She'd never forget those eyes glaring back at her from the rearview mirror. Instinctively she took a step back.

"That's him," she whispered.

Detective Fandino glanced at Kane, then back to Allison. "Are you sure?"

She looked at the man again. It was Charles Harlan. She felt a shiver run through her. "Yes. I'm sure."

The detective smiled. "That's all I wanted to hear."

Relief flooded through Allison. It *was* Harlan. They had him. Behind bars. She was safe now. *Safe.*

When Detective Fandino moved away to speak with another officer in the room, Allison turned to look at Kane. He was still staring through the window into the other room, his jaw tightly clenched, as he watched Harlan being escorted from the room.

She watched Harlan glare at a police officer as cuffs were locked onto his hands. She stared at the man and felt a mixture of anger and bitterness, but also, in a strange way, almost a sense of gratitude that if only for a short time he'd brought Kane into her life.

"What's going to happen now?" she asked, rubbing her arms as she turned back to Kane.

Kane watched until the door closed behind Harlan. "There's a long list of people who want this guy. There'll be extradition requests from at least three different states. By the time he gets out of jail—if he ever does—they'll have to push him out in a wheelchair."

Over. It was finally over. She blinked back the tears of relief. She could move back into her own apartment. Return to work. Go where she wanted, when she wanted, without worrying about kidnapping; without security guards watching her every move. Without Kane.

An emptiness settled over her. There was no reason for him to stay any longer. He'd done his job and he'd done it well. Case closed.

She'd known the time would come, but she never could have prepared herself for the pain that came with it.

"We're finished here now, Miss Westcott," Detective Fandino said. "If we need anything else, we'll call."

Kane shook hands with the man and thanked him. The rain was just starting when they stepped outside the police station.

"I'd like to stop by the center on the way home," she

said flatly, hurrying toward the car. "I haven't seen the kids in four days, and I'm sure you'd like to say goodbye."

"Allison."

He took her arm and held her still. They stood there, in the light rain staring at each other. Thunder rumbled close by. "What?" she asked quietly. A faint light of hope rose in her as she watched him struggle to speak.

"I—I'll miss the kids."

Her heart sank. "They'll miss you, too." And *she* would miss him. God, how she'd miss him.

He started to say something else, but a bolt of lightning, followed by a loud crack of thunder stopped him. He pulled her to the car and opened the door, then quickly closed it after she got in.

They were silent on the way to the center. Allison stared out the window while Kane concentrated on the rain-slick road. At one point, she glanced behind the van, looking for Tony, but realized he wasn't there. It was no longer necessary. He'd go back to his regular routine, as she would go back to hers. Business as usual, she thought dryly.

By the time they got to the center, it was raining hard enough for Allison to retrieve her umbrella out of the back seat. Though she rarely used it, she was glad now that she had it. It gave her something to hold on to as she and Kane walked across the parking lot.

"I need to talk with the director for a few minutes," Allison told Kane as they stepped into the hallway. "Why don't you go see Billy now?"

"You aren't coming with me?"

If the ache in her chest hadn't been so sharp, Allison might have laughed at the surprise—and fear—in Kane's eyes. He was a man who put his life on the line every day of his life, yet he was obviously terrified to say goodbye to one little boy.

She shook her head slowly. "You're on your own, Kane."

Kane watched Allison walk away and the impact of her words left a hollowness inside him he'd never experienced before. He'd always been on his own. He was used to being on his own.

The door to Billy's room was open. He sat at a desk in the corner, working at a model of a stealth bomber that Kane had given him a few days ago.

Kane dragged in a deep breath and knocked lightly on the door.

"Kane!" Billy's face broke into a wide grin. "Come see what I've done."

Kane moved beside Billy and examined the model. It was almost completed, and Kane felt a strange sense of pride that the boy had put it together almost entirely by himself.

"You're going to make a great engineer some day," Kane said, smiling down at the youngster.

Billy shook his head. "I'm not going to build them. I'm going to fly them."

Something told Kane that Billy's affirmation would come true. And even though it would be a few years away, Kane would make sure that Billy at least got a chance when the time came.

"Is Allison back?" Billy asked suddenly, looking back toward the door.

"Yes, she's—"

"Why didn't she come see me?"

The look of disappointment on Billy's face cut sharply through Kane's chest. "She...well, she thought I might want a minute alone with you to, uh, talk with you."

"About what?"

Dammit, dammit, dammit. There had to be an easier way. But there wasn't. *So just say it.*

"I came to say goodbye."

Billy was quiet for a long moment as he stared up into Kane's face. A shuttered look fell over the child's dark brown eyes. "You're leaving?"

Kane nodded. "I was working on a job for Allison's father, but I'm finished now."

"Can't you get another job?"

"My job isn't like other people's," Kane said hesitantly. "I travel all over. I'm gone most of the time."

"Why?"

Why? It was a simple question, one only a child could ask. A question that suddenly Kane didn't have an answer to.

Or maybe he did have the answer. And he was too damn afraid to recognize it.

"We can keep in touch." Kane shoved his hands into his pockets. "I can call you."

Billy put the cap on the glue and stood. "Sure. That would be fine."

Kane knew that Billy didn't believe him. It was obvious in his eyes. How many people had lied to this child? His own mother had told him she was coming back and she hadn't.

"Billy, it's not like—"

"I'd really like to go see Allison now," Billy said, cutting Kane off. "Goodbye."

Billy walked from the room without looking back. As he watched him go, Kane understood why he hated goodbyes so much. They hurt.

Kane looked around Billy's room, saw the stark walls

and the meager belongings. Except for the model, there was nothing here that was Billy's. It was a room that had belonged to dozens of kids before him and would belong to dozens more after he was gone. He'd never feel as if he belonged. Anywhere or to anyone.

The tightness in Kane's chest surprised him. He'd left those feelings behind him long ago. He was a man now. He'd survived those rough years. So would Billy.

Who the hell was he kidding?

With a heavy sigh, Kane stared blankly at the cold tile floor. He'd spent a lifetime running away from those feelings. He'd never left them behind. Hell, he'd never even admitted them.

Not until now. Not until Allison.

He could see her easy smile, hear her soft laugh. She'd turned many a head with her beauty, but it was what was inside her that Kane knew he'd fallen in love with. She gave of herself, selflessly, and asked for nothing in return. It was a rare quality. One to be treasured and cherished.

For the first time in his life he was so close. Close to belonging, to being wanted.

It scared the hell out of him.

He needed to talk with her. He hadn't a clue what he'd say, but he desperately wanted her to understand. The only problem was, *he* didn't understand.

And instinctively Kane knew that the only person who could help him with that was Billy.

He walked into the hall. It was empty. Most of the children were in the game room, listening to a story being read. Kane found Allison in the crafts room, helping a little girl with red hair cut out paper hearts. They were singing a song about an elephant named Elvis. He stood there watching her, feeling as if he was drowning and the past few days of his life were passing before his eyes. In his mind, he saw Allison. Defiant when he'd told her to stay home from the center. Determined when they'd worked on her lessons. Indignant when he bullied her. She'd held him in her arms, touched him with her hands and her heart, then met him face on, never once backing down from him.

Allison looked up at him when he moved beside her. Her voice faltered on the final chorus when he reached over her and picked up a paper heart from the table. Strange, he thought, how heavy the piece of paper felt in his hand. The little girl continued to sing by herself as she glued the hearts on a piece of paper.

"Have you seen Billy?" he asked.

Allison stood and hugged the little girl, then walked into the hall. "I thought he was with you."

Kane shook his head impatiently. "He came looking for you."

With a sigh, Allison pulled her hands through her hair. "I'll check the back rooms and the parking lot," she said. "You look in the dining room and front yard."

His face sullen, Kane hurried off. How strange, Allison thought. She was actually giving Kane instructions for a change. And he actually did as she said.

She checked all of the rooms in the back of the center, but Billy wasn't there. Which left the parking lot. She grabbed her umbrella on the way out the back door. She'd known he'd take Kane's leaving hard. She couldn't fault him for wanting a few minutes alone.

It was raining hard. Large drops pounded on the metal awnings over the back windows. A mist rose up from the asphalt parking lot.

"Billy?" She walked toward the corner, fumbling with

the catch on the umbrella. There was a small shed on the side of the building. He might have gone in there.

"Billy?" she called his name again. "It's Allison. I want to—"

A man grabbed her arm as she rounded the corner and threw her against the side of the house. The breath whooshed out of her lungs from the impact. Before she could gather air to scream, a large hand covered her mouth.

"One sound and you're dead," the man hissed. A knife glinted close to her neck. He lowered his face to hers and Allison felt the scream tear silently at her throat.

His eyes. The same eyes from the rearview mirror.

Harlan's eyes.

Twelve

Kane closed the door behind him and stepped out onto the front porch. Rain poured from the roof gutter, splashing loudly into the dirt bed beside the porch steps. Soaking wet, Billy sat at the bottom of the steps, elbows on his knees, mindlessly tapping his tennis shoes in a big puddle.

Relief that Billy was all right surged through Kane. He started to tell the boy to come in out of the rain, but instead he sat down beside him. "Okay if I sit here?"

Billy nodded, but kept his gaze directed downward.

Kane's heart gave a twist as he realized why Billy was sitting in the rain: to hide his tears.

Kane had never felt so helpless in his entire life. Helpless and inadequate and unqualified. He had no idea what to say.

"Allison's worried about you," Kane said finally, but the words didn't feel right.

"I'm okay." Billy picked up a pebble and tossed it into the puddle.

"*I'm* worried about you." That felt better.

Billy glanced sideways at Kane. "Why?"

Why? Why did kids always ask *why?* And why was it always so damn hard to answer them?

Kane had trained himself to think fast, to analyze a situation and react. Logic. Reason. Control. Those were the things he understood. What he knew.

But logic and reason had no place here with Billy.

Honesty. That's what Billy needed.

That's what everyone needed.

They sat there for a long moment, the rain beating down on them, both of them silent.

Finally Kane said, "I'm not leaving because I want to, Billy. It's just that I, well, I have to."

Billy reached for a small stick and drew lines in the wet dirt. "That's what my mom said."

Kane closed his eyes, stunned by the sharpness of the pain that cut through him. "Sometimes people make bad choices when they're confused or scared. It doesn't mean she doesn't love you."

Billy thought carefully about that. "She thought she might have to go to jail. I guess that's pretty scary."

Kane felt an anger rise in him at Billy's mother. She ran out on her only kid, probably the only person in her life who really loved her, just so she could save her own neck.

And then it hit Kane with the force of a lightning bolt: He was running out on the only person *he'd* ever loved. The only person who'd ever loved him. Allison. And wasn't it for the same reason? To save his own neck? Because he was scared?

What a fool he'd been. He only prayed it wasn't too late to set things right.

Billy swiped at the rain dripping from his forehead. "Kane, can I call you sometime? Maybe when I get scared?"

"We can do better than that," Kane said and a feeling so profound and so overwhelming swelled up inside him that he could no longer speak. *We can do much better than that.*

And then he did something he'd seen Allison do time and time again. Something he hadn't thought he could do.

He hugged Billy.

It felt strange at first. Billy sat, unmoving, his hands at his sides. And then slowly Billy's arms came up and circled Kane's waist. It no longer felt strange.

It felt like home.

Think! Think! Allison's mind raced. *Never panic.* Kane's words echoed in her mind. This man couldn't be Charles Harlan. She'd left him at the police station less than thirty minutes ago. This *had* to be a different man.

But who?

The brother. Harlan's brother. Nick Harlan. She knew that Kane had a man watching him in Chicago, but obviously he had managed to get away. The rain plastered his dark hair to his head and dripped off, giving his face the appearance of melting wax. He was smaller than his brother, but wider in the shoulders and neck.

He eased his wet hand from her mouth, but the knife hovered close by her throat. If she screamed, she'd be dead.

"Now," he said roughly, "you and me are going to take a little ride."

"The police already have your brother and his friend."

She forced her voice to remain calm, but inside she was shaking. "They're looking for you now," she lied.

His laugh was gravelly. "You and me both know that's not true, now, don't we? No one even knows I'm in Seattle."

She had to stall for time. Keep him talking. *Please, Kane. Look for me.* "Rhonda knew. She told the police about you."

Uncertainty narrowed his dark eyes, then he shook his head. "Rhonda thinks I'm still in Chicago." He twisted the knife in his hand. "I'll settle with that bitch later for turning Charlie and Brad in to the cops." He leaned closer, and the smell of stale cigarette smoke made Allison's stomach turn. "After you and me finish our business."

"It's over," Allison said with more self-confidence than she felt. "Get out now. While you still can."

She gasped in pain as he shoved her against the wall with his forearm. "Charlie had it all figured out. Where to stash you, a safe place for the ransom pickup. Even a way out of the country. It's too sweet a deal to walk away from, lady. Now that you ain't got your watchdogs no more, getting money from your daddy will be like taking candy from a baby."

He grabbed her arm with bruising force and dragged her away from the wall, toward an open van. She slipped on the wet pavement and stumbled when he shoved her forward, but she managed to stay on her feet. He held the knife to her back, jabbing it at her shoulder blade. A few more feet and he'd have her....

No. There was no way. It was going to end, and it was going to end here. Now.

Gripping the umbrella still in her hand, Allison spun sharply to her left, bringing the umbrella around and knocking the man's arm away. Without hesitation, she yelled and kicked out, catching him square in the groin. With a loud moan, he dropped the knife from his hand as he doubled over.

Allison turned to run, but his hand shot out, catching her leg. She went down, landing hard on her bad knee. Stars flew in front of her eyes. Swearing, he dragged her closer to him, reaching for the knife that lay only inches away.

Ignoring the white-hot pain shooting through her knee and leg, Allison clenched her right hand into a fist. With her middle knuckle extended, she smashed her hand into the man's temple. He screamed in pain, releasing his grip on her leg.

Run! Run! she yelled silently, but when she tried to stand, her knee gave out. She crumpled on the wet pavement, struggling to crawl away.

She turned to look back, and it seemed as if she were watching a motion picture, frame by frame. The reach of the man's arm. The gargled sound of the swear word from his mouth. The look of pure hatred as his fingers closed around the knife. Even the rain felt as if it were in slow motion. She felt each drop splatter against her face and roll away.

The man raised his arm. Swung the knife toward her…

A cry of pure outrage shook the air. A long, muscular leg shot across her line of vision and knocked the knife from the man's hand. A second swinging kick a split second later caught him smack in the jaw. Stunned, the man's eyes widened, then closed. He fell forward, face first, and landed on the pavement with a dull thud.

Kane.

"Allison!"

Too dazed to answer, Allison lay back, watching the tall figure of the man she loved kneel beside her.

Thank God. Thank God.

"It's about time you got here," was all she could manage to whisper.

She stood at the edge of the cliff, staring out across the water, watching the white-tipped waves lap on the beach below. The rain had stopped about an hour earlier, but dark and threatening clouds still hung low, promising to unleash another torrent at a moment's notice.

The air always smelled so clean after a storm, Allison thought, drawing the scent of damp earth and wet fir into her lungs. Normally after it rained she would feel a sense of renewal, of invigoration.

But today was hardly what she would consider normal.

Over and over, the scenario ran through her mind. Nick Harlan's hand on her leg, dragging her toward him…his eyes shining with hatred as he raised the knife….

And then Kane.

Shivering, she pulled her sweater tightly around her. She couldn't think about what would have happened if he hadn't shown up when he had. He *had* shown up. That's all that mattered.

After he'd picked her up and carried her back into the center, Allison hadn't caught more than a glimpse of Kane the rest of the afternoon. He'd been busy outside with the police and after the paramedics wrapped her knee and treated a few scratches, Tony suddenly appeared and insisted he drive her home.

She knew, of course, that Tony was following Kane's instructions. To make everyone's life easier, and because she simply hadn't the strength to argue, she went with him.

He was watching her now, leaning casually against a fir tree several yards away. When she glanced back to look at him, a gust of wind picked up, showering water and fir needles on him. He jumped at the unexpected downpour, then swore as he brushed himself off.

Grinning, she turned away and looked out over the sound. A speedboat some distance off loped across the water and the hum of its motor drifted on the cool breeze.

Tony had been the one to suggest they take a walk out here, and though she'd been reluctant, he'd insisted the fresh air would do her good. Now, as she watched a large brown pelican skim gracefully over the water, she was glad she'd given in to his gentle persuasion. She felt composed again. Calmer.

She knew the nightmare was truly over now. With both the Harlan brothers behind bars, she had no reason to be afraid any longer. She knew it was time to put her life back together.

A breeze picked up the ends of her hair, tossing them about her face. With a sigh she tucked them back, and the simple gesture reminded her of Kane, how he'd combed his fingers through her hair after they'd made love. He was a man capable of incredible tenderness and compassion, and at the same time capable of fierce violence.

What he wasn't capable of, she thought bitterly, was recognizing that he had the ability to love. To love and be loved. The risk was too great for him. It was the one thing that scared the hell out of him.

She'd seen how difficult it had been for him to say goodbye not only to her but to Billy as well. She felt a certain sense of satisfaction in knowing that it hadn't been easy, but that hadn't helped ease the pain.

But pain, though she certainly didn't like it, was something she was going to have to get used to.

The speedboat drew closer and she squinted her eyes, watching its approach. It wasn't one of the neighbors'. She would have recognized the boat if it were. The beach here was private. No one belonged out here.

She expected the boat to turn away, but instead it drove onto the beach. A man wearing a hooded blue rain slicker jumped out and started up the short path toward her.

She felt a moment of panic, then recognized the powerful shoulders and determined walk.

Kane?

Why in the world had he driven a boat here?

She turned to question Tony, but he was gone.

But she knew why Kane was here. The only reason he would be here.

To say goodbye.

She folded her arms tightly, watching him approach. She thought he looked like a fisherman coming home after a long day's work, and remembered their own fishing expedition in the mountains. It was the only time they'd truly been alone, without the rest of the world intruding. They'd laughed together, made love. And even as short as that time had been, she knew she'd never forget one minute of it.

He stopped two feet away from her and pulled down the hood of his slicker. His eyes were intense, his face serious. "How you feeling?"

He meant physically. What else was there for him? *Damn you, Thomas Kane.* "I'm fine."

He looked past her, toward the house, then returned his gaze to hers. "You did good today, Allison. Nick Harlan will be singing soprano for a long time." Kane smiled.

"When the police handcuffed him, he complained that his 'jewels were shattered.'"

It was still hard for her to believe she'd actually kicked the man where she had. She hadn't even thought. She'd just done it. "I had a good teacher. A bully, but good, nonetheless."

He moved closer, so close she could smell the ocean on his skin, see the fine lines of fatigue around his blue eyes. "I almost made a big mistake today, Allison. A mistake that could have cost lives."

Of course it would bother Kane that he'd made a mistake, she thought sadly. He was a man who demanded as much from himself as he did from others. And he would take the blame, whether it was his or not. "You had no way of knowing that Nick Harlan was part of his brother's plot."

"I'm not talking about Nick Harlan," he said quietly. "I'm talking about us. About our lives together and the fact that I almost let you get away from me."

Allison's heart sped up and hammered in her chest, as if she'd been running up a long, steep hill. And that's exactly what she should do. Run. As fast and as far away from this man as she could. How many times did she have to touch fire before she understood that it burned? No, she wasn't going to make a fool out of herself again. She didn't dare hope....

Did she?

Arms folded, she faced him. "Keep talking."

Kane knew she wouldn't make this easy for him. And why should she? After what he'd put her through, what he'd put them *both* through. He wouldn't blame her if she threw him off the cliff.

He racked his brain to find the right words, desperately

wanting her to understand. *To understand what?* Hell, *he* didn't understand.

But for the first time in his life he was going to think and talk with his heart, not his head. Now, if only Allison was listening. He took a deep breath and just said it.

"I love you."

"What did you say?" Her voice was no more than a whisper on the breeze.

It hadn't been as difficult as he'd thought. In fact, it felt good. Very good. "I love you."

Allison swore to herself that she would be calm. Isn't that what Kane had taught her? Not to panic in a life-threatening situation?

And that's exactly what this was. Life threatening. Because if he walked away now, after telling her he loved her, she knew it would kill her. "Why are you telling me this?"

Kane stared at Allison. She wasn't giving him an inch here. Nor did he deserve it. "I've been alone since I was seven, Allison. No one helped me through my nightmares and no one ever put an arm around me to ease the pain. I dealt with that emptiness the only way I knew how. I became a master at control. My life, my actions, my feelings. I was alone, and I'd convinced myself I liked it that way. There was nothing and no one who had power over me." He looked down at her, at her deep green eyes and the wild mass of chestnut curls surrounding her face. "And then you walked into your father's office."

With a sigh, he dragged his hands through his damp hair. "From that moment, the control I'd prided myself on was shattered into a thousand pieces. I felt like a teenager again. Awkward and unsure and completely inept. It made me furious. But even more, it scared the hell out of me.

"And somewhere between that day you handed Billy a

Game Mania and this morning when you were singing about an elephant named Elvis, I fell completely and irrevocably in love with you.''

He reached out to tuck a stray curl behind her ear. She closed her eyes when his fingertips brushed over her skin, then opened them again, but she said nothing. She was waiting, he knew it. He sucked in a deep breath and his heart was pounding so hard he thought it might explode. *Just say it.* ''I want you to marry me.''

Marry him? Allison was still struggling to absorb Kane's admission of love. And now he was asking her to marry him? She took a step closer, closing the gap between them, then lifted her face to his and looked him in the eye. ''Five minutes ago,'' she said quietly, ''I thought I'd never see you again. You've shut me out, hurt me and bullied me. Now you expect me to *marry* you?''

This was hardly going the way he'd planned. Would he ever understand Allison? Probably not, but he had the rest of his life to work on it. ''Yes.''

''Yes?'' She gestured wide. ''All you can say is yes?''

''Well, there is one other thing.''

She folded her arms. ''And what's that?''

He hesitated on this one. After all, it was a lot to throw out at her at one time. ''I want Billy to come live with us.''

Surprise—or maybe something closer to shock—registered on Allison's face. She stood there, stunned, her jaw slack.

And then she started to cry.

Panic began a slow rise in Kane. She didn't want him. He'd pushed her too far and he'd lost her. The thought terrified him. ''Maybe you need to think about this a while,'' he said and the words were like sandpaper in his throat. In the meantime, he had a bottle of whiskey he'd promised his attention to several weeks ago.

He started to turn away, but a need more powerful than his own pride had him turning back and pulling her into his arms. With a fierce desperation, he covered her mouth with his, tilting her head back as he kissed her hard.

"Marry me," he said roughly, brushing her cheeks with his lips. He tasted the salt of her tears and his fear of losing her overwhelmed him. "Don't think about it. Just say you will. Please."

Allison was finding it impossible to say *anything*. She wound her arms tightly around Kane's neck, fighting back a fresh burst of tears. She pressed her lips to his, letting her kiss answer for her.

He pulled away sharply, holding her at arm's length. His eyes were dark and intense. "Tell me that was a yes."

"Yes," she whispered.

"Tell me you love me."

She smiled. That was the easiest thing he'd ever asked her to do. "I love you, Thomas Kane. I love you."

He kissed her again, long and slow, slanting his mouth to fit hers perfectly. His tongue slid over hers again and again and she felt dizzy with the sensations swirling through her. *He loved her, wanted to marry her. And Billy...*

Billy.

She pressed her hands on Kane's chest and pushed away. "Tell me about Billy again."

He loosened his hold on her and gazed softly down at her. "I want him to come live with us."

"Does he know about this?"

Kane shook his head. "I wanted us to tell him together. But I did make a couple of calls to set the wheels in motion.

Because of his age, there shouldn't be any problems. We could take him home with us before the week is out.'' Concern furrowed Kane's brow. ''If you agree, of course.''

Home with us. She'd never heard a more wonderful phrase. She knew there'd be rough spots for all of them, but then, when it came to Kane, that was a given. ''This is a scary thought, Kane, but for the first time since I've met you, I agree with you completely.''

He raised one eyebrow. ''Are you trying to tell me I'm difficult?''

''Of course not. Stubborn, obstinate and demanding are a much better choice of words.''

He laughed softly and kissed her nose. ''All we have to decide now is where 'home' is.''

Now *that* was something they were going to have to talk about. Florida was a million miles from Seattle. ''Kane, you know I can't—''

Knowing what she was going to say, he cut her off. ''I can headquarter my business anywhere. And besides, I even think I've come to like the rain.'' Several drops were starting to fall now. ''Who knows, maybe I'll put Tony in charge and take his job at your father's company.''

That would be the day. Laughing, she slipped her arms around his neck, then suddenly pulled away. ''That reminds me. Where *is* Tony? He was standing a few yards away before you got here.'' Her brow furrowed. ''And why in the world did you drive up in a boat?''

''Plan B.''

''Plan B?''

''If you said no.''

She narrowed her eyes and took a step back. ''What if I had said no?''

His smile was almost sinister. "Then I was going to kid-nap you."

"What?"

"Kidnap you." His smile widened and he moved toward her. "In fact, I still like plan B."

She didn't like the gleam in his eyes at all. *He wouldn't dare.* "Kane, I don't know what you're—"

He moved so quickly she hadn't time to even turn. She shrieked as he tossed her over his shoulder.

With a mixture of outrage and laughter, she screamed at him to put her down. He ignored her and headed down the short path toward the beach.

"I have to warn you, mister," she yelled at him. "These hands are trained to kill."

"You can show me later," he called back. He already had images of those hands moving over his body when he got her alone. He knew it would take exactly thirty-seven minutes to reach the forty-foot cabin cruiser moored at Gig Harbor. He'd called in a favor for a two-day loan of the boat and had no intention of wasting one minute.

"Kane! Put me down!"

"Not a chance, Allison." He held her tighter.

Laughing, she grabbed his shoulders to balance herself. Was this what it would be like with Kane? Wild and un-certain? Reckless and unpredictable?

She certainly hoped so, Allison thought with a smile. She certainly hoped so.

And as they bounced down the path toward the waiting boat, she held on to him for dear life.

* * * * *

HARLEQUIN® *Romance*

A family saga begins to unravel
when the doors to the Bella Lucia
Restaurant Empire are opened...

*A family torn apart by secrets,
reunited by marriage*

AUGUST 2006

Meet Rachel Valentine, in
HAVING THE FRENCHMAN'S BABY
by Rebecca Winters

Find out what happens when a night of passion is followed
by a shocking revelation and an unexpected pregnancy!

SEPTEMBER 2006

The Valentine family saga continues with
THE REBEL PRINCE by Raye Morgan